When Geoffrey McSkimming was a boy he
found an old motion-picture projector and a tin
containing a dusty film in his grandmother's attic.
He screened the film and was transfixed by
the flickering image of a man in a jaunty pith helmet,
baggy Sahara shorts and special desert sun-spectacles.
The man had an imposing macaw and a clever-looking
camel, and Geoffrey McSkimming was mesmerized
by their activities in black-and-white Egypt, Peru,
Greece, and other exotic locations.

Years later he discovered the identities of the trio,
and he has spent much of his time since then retracing
their footsteps, interviewing surviving members of the
Old Relics Society, and gradually reconstructing these
lost true tales which have become the enormously
successful Cairo Jim Chronicles.

Geoffrey McSkimming would like to thank the
members of the Old Relic Society in Cairo, Egypt,
who assisted him with much of the factual
information contained in this story.

This story is for BBY,
once again with all my love

We have lingered in the chambers of the sea.
T. S. Eliot

CAIRO JIM

AND THE SUNKEN
SARCOPHAGUS OF SEKHERET

A Tale of Mayhem, Mystery
and Moisture

GEOFFREY McSKIMMING

WALKER
BOOKS

This is a work of fiction. Names, characters, places, and incidents are
either products of the author's imagination or, if real, are used fictitiously.

First published in Great Britain 2006 by Walker Books Ltd
87 Vauxhall Walk, London SE11 5HJ

2 4 6 8 10 9 7 5 3 1

Text © 1994 Geoffrey McSkimming
Cover illustration © 2006 Martin Chatterton

The right of Geoffrey McSkimming to be identified as author of
this work has been asserted by him in accordance with the
Copyright, Designs and Patents Act 1988.

This book has been typeset in Plantin

Printed in Great Britain by
Cox & Wyman Ltd, Reading, Berkshire

British Library Cataloguing in Publication Data:
a catalogue record for this book is available from the British Library.

ISBN-13: 978-1-4063-0021-5
ISBN-10: 1-4063-0021-7

www.walkerbooks.co.uk

▲▲▲▲▲▲ CONTENTS ▲▲▲▲▲▲

A WORD TO MY READERS

In 1838, when people had little regard or respect for the histories and cultures of other countries, a dreadful thing happened. The golden sarcophagus of Menkaure, Pharaoh of Egypt, was loaded onto a boat bound for the British Museum in London. It was never to arrive: not long out to sea, a mighty storm blew up from nowhere and shipwrecked the vessel, depositing the royal casket somewhere at the bottom of the ocean.

Several years ago, while researching more of the Cairo Jim Chronicles, I made a startling discovery – that the incident involving Pharaoh Menkaure's sarcophagus was not the first occasion when such a thing had occurred. A short time before the sinking of Menkaure, another royal sarcophagus had met a similar fate.

Had it not been for the efforts of that well-known archaeologist and little-known poet, Cairo Jim, and his friends Doris the macaw and Brenda the Wonder Camel, and the co-operation of Gerald Perry Esquire of the Old Relics Society in Cairo (the gentleman who told much of it to me), I would not have the following tale to tell...

G. McS.

Part One:

FELONIOUS
SUBMERGENCE

A TRICK OF THE LIGHT

IT WAS THE PERFECT DAY for reading.

Brenda the Wonder Camel was lying outside the Amun-Ra Tea Rooms in Luxor, Upper Egypt, with the drowsy sunlight tingling her eyelashes. Her rear legs were crossed comfortably, and in front of her, propped up against a rock and opened for her to read, was the latest Melodious Tex western adventure novel, *Melodious Tex and the Mystery of the Terpsichorean Cows.*

Next to the book sat a plate of freshly turned earthworms which Mrs Amun-Ra, the stout and friendly proprietress of the establishment, had been thoughtful enough to provide especially for Brenda, and the immensely contented Wonder Camel was enjoying these almost as much as her story. Every few pages or so she would suck one up, spaghetti-fashion, and it would disappear with a loud Bactrian slurp.

She was in the middle of Chapter Four – where the musical cowboy Melodious Tex and the Sheriff of Chinless Gulch were about to blow up the empty hideout of the villain, Malodorous Denzil (rustler and cow-slapper) – when her concentration was broken by a sudden exclamation from the open-air dining courtyard behind her.

"Well, swoggle me sideways with a sphinx's head-dress," blurted Cairo Jim, rather loudly for a public place.

Brenda looked up to where her archaeologist-poet friend was sitting beneath a shady palm tree, reading *The Egyptian Gazette*. On a perch nearby, her other friend, the yellow-and-blue macaw known as Doris, stopped eating her snail cakes and blinked at him. "Raark. What's up, Jim?" Doris squawked.

"Well, I'll be—" muttered Jim, staring at the newspaper.

"What is it? Tell me!" Doris moved her neck up and down, her brow feathers creased with impatience.

Mrs Amun-Ra, having also heard the exclamation, came bustling out of the kitchen, carrying a plate full of little round pink cakes. "Mr Jim, Mr Jim, what is mattering? You sound as though your flabber has been gasted! Is your tea too hot? Is there not enough lemon in it?"

"It's something he's read in the newspaper," answered Doris, opening her wings and closing them.

"Oh?" said Mrs Amun-Ra.

"Listen to this," Jim said, half-distractedly. He cleared his throat and read aloud the headline which had so startled him:

"'HUGE AQUATIC BEAST SEEN ON RED SEA'." His eyes were wide behind his desert sun-spectacles.

"Aquatic beast?" said Mrs Amun-Ra. "Whatever could it be?"

"Raark," said Doris.

"I've no idea," pondered Jim. "Listen to what's happened—"

Mrs Amun-Ra cocked her head towards him. "I'm all ears, Mr Jim."

"I'm all feathers," said Doris.

For the eighth time in the past fortnight, local residents of the village of Hurghada have reported seeing a large, black, serpent-like beast upon the surface of the Red Sea. It has appeared at the same time on every occasion, at nine p.m. precisely, and has proceeded to swim silently up and down a small area, never venturing out of its circular course. Then, at ten thirty-three p.m. precisely, the beast changes its tack and floats off towards the south, where it has repeatedly disappeared into the night.

"Goodness gracious," said Mrs Amun-Ra.

Doris hopped from her perch and onto Jim's shoulder. "Does it say how big it is?" she asked.

"Yes," nodded Jim:

Eyewitnesses claim the beast is about the size of an autobus. It has a long neck, similar to that of a giraffe, and a head shaped like a horse's. Its body shape, visible above the water, is round, with a prominent hump in the middle of its back.

"Quaaaoo." Brenda, who had been eavesdropping,

snorted at the mention of the hump.

"It sounds like another Loch Ness Monstrosity," said Mrs Amun-Ra, pulling out a chair next to Jim and sitting.

Jim turned to her. "You may be right, Mrs A."

"Loch Ness Monstrosity?" Doris screeched. "What, pray tell, is this "Loch Ness Monstrosity"?"

"The Loch Ness Monster," explained Jim, "is an enormous creature which has been regularly spied on Loch Ness in Scotland."

"A country to which I have not yet been," blinked the macaw.

Mrs Amun-Ra leaned forward and whispered in what she imagined was a sinister manner. "They say it is some ancient thing that has existed undisturbed on the bottoms of the water. Those lochs are very deep, you know. They think that the Loch Ness Monstrosity might be *prehysterical*!"

"Prehistoric," nodded Cairo Jim.

"Yes," said Mrs Amun-Ra. "It could be a Tyrablosaurus named Rex!"

"Look, Mrs A." Jim showed her the newspaper. "Here's a drawing of the Hurghada beast. An artist's impression, of course. You're right; it does look very similar to Nessie."

Mrs Amun-Ra and Doris peered at the illustration.

"What a beastie," Doris chirped.

"I would not like to bump into her while I was taking a drip," shuddered Mrs Amun-Ra.

"It looks like it could chomp a bit of a bite out of

 **12**

one, doesn't it?"

Mrs Amun-Ra squirmed in her chair.

At that point Brenda the Wonder Camel lifted her head from Melodious Tex. She felt the sun's warmth against her mane and upon her ears, and (for no other reason than that she was a Wonder Camel) she gently thought the name Sekheret.

An instant later, her thought had travelled along the soft beams of sunlight between her and Jim, and he looked up with a start.

"Sekheret?" he said, quite out of the blue.

"Sekheret?" repeated Doris.

"Oh, no, Mr Jim." Mrs Amun-Ra held up her hands. "I do not smoke, you should know that."

"No, Mrs A, *Sekheret*. The obscure Pharaoh of the Twenty-third Dynasty."

"Reerk," nodded Doris.

Brenda went back to her book.

"I do not overstand," Mrs Amun-Ra said, looking blank.

"Why," said Jim, "it just occurred to me that the area where this beast is being spotted – off the coast of Hurghada – is in roughly the same vicinity where the golden sarcophagus of the Pharaoh Sekheret was lost at sea in 1832."

"Lost at sea?" asked Mrs Amun-Ra. "How could such a thing happen? A *Pharaoh* lost at sea? Preponderous!"

"Rerark, it was a most unfortunate incident," flapped

Doris, who, since Jim had met her in Peru and brought her back to Egypt*, had studied Egyptian archaeology with an interest bordering on obsession. "They should never have been allowed to get away with it," she huffed.

"You're too right, my dear," frowned Cairo Jim.

"Get away with it? *Who* got away with it? *Who* got away with *what*?" Mrs Amun-Ra wiped her brow with the hem of her apron.

"Mrs A, unfortunately my profession has not always been swathed in integrity. There was a time, not so very long ago in fact, when foreign archaeologists would come into this magnificent land—"

"Ah," smiled Mrs Amun-Ra, her bosom swelling with inflating pride.

"—and, once they had discovered the great treasures of antiquity they were seeking, they would promptly skedaddle, taking with them whatever they had unearthed. It was common practice, and the foreign governments of the day would often encourage these so-called archaeologists."

"Encourage them?"

"Raark," nodded Doris. "Even to the point of funding their expeditions."

"How very rude and callow!" Mrs Amun-Ra was clearly shocked. "You mean to say, Mr Jim, that these people – I shall not insult you by calling them

* See *Cairo Jim on the Trail to ChaCha Muchos* (An Epic Tale of Rhythm).

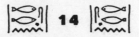

'archaeologists' – took away my country's her
Pieces of our history?"

"That's what happened, I'm afraid."

Mrs Amun-Ra clenched her hands into tight balls.
"Plunderers!" she exploded. "Pillowers!"

"And that's what happened to the sarcophagus of
Pharaoh Sekheret. Or rather, what was *meant* to happen
to it. You see, nature decided to take a different course."

"Tell me, please, Mr Jim."

Cairo Jim placed his newspaper on the table and
took a sip of tea. "It was all because of Sir Murray
Savlon," he explained. "He was, in the early nineteenth
century, a noted adventurer with a well-publicised lust
for gold. His passion was rather like that of our own
Captain Neptune Bone, you might say—"

At the sound of the name of Jim's arch rival, Doris
gave an ear-rocketing screech and flapped her wings in a
feathered frenzy. "*Reerraarrk!*"

"Steady on, my dear," soothed Jim. "No one knows
where Captain Bone is, remember? He's gone to
ground, in hiding."

"He'll turn up again, like a bad piastre. Evil of his
kind always does."

Jim patted her crest and turned back to Mrs Amun-
Ra. "Well, Mrs A, Sir Murray Savlon's desire for gold
brought him to Egypt in search of the gold casket
containing Pharaoh Sekheret. He began digging in the
Valley of the Kings in 1830, but he soon gave that up
when he heard that Sekheret had been entombed in an

elaborate bent pyramid by the shores of the Red Sea. He packed up all his workers and their tools and dominoes and off they went to what is now the region around Hurghada. Here they recommenced their search.

"After nearly two years, he and his workers discovered what was left of the pyramid. There wasn't much, most of it having crumbled beneath the many layers of sand that covered it like layers of icing on a cake. Digging further, they were fortunate enough to find the burial chamber and, eventually, the dazzling sarcophagus itself. After they'd brought it to the surface of the earth and dusted it off, it looked as perfect and bright and golden as the day it was formed."

"And then?" said Mrs Amun-Ra. "What took place following this?"

"Savlon had the casket loaded onto his ship, the *Vanderdecken* and, not three hours out to sea, they were besieged by a ferocious storm. The maelstrom was said to be so very fierce it lifted the entire ship out of the water as though it were a mere twig. The 0 was soon splintered asunder, and both halves sank, groaning, into the turbulent depths." Jim frowned and lowered his voice. "The sarcophagus of Sekheret went with them, to a watery niche we know not where."

Mrs Amun-Ra sighed and shook her head. "Ah, the folly of ambition."

"And greed," added Jim.

"'Is't possible?'" squawked Doris in a declamatory fashion. "'No sooner got but lost?' Raaark! *Troilus and*

Cressida by Mr Shakespeare. Act IV, Scene 2."

Jim smiled. "Very good, Doris."

The noble macaw's beak wrinkled at the edges.

Mrs Amun-Ra looked at the illustration in the newspaper. "I wonder if our beastie knows of the King lying so far below?"

"I wonder what our beastie *is*," said Jim, stroking his chin with his thumb.

"Rerk," rerked Doris.

"Here, Mr Jim. Do not worry about such things. You will only get indiscretion." Mrs Amun-Ra plonked her plate of tiny pink cakes on the newspaper. "Scoff a few of these pinkies, they will take your mind off beasties and underwater Pharaohs. I've just baked the hugest batch for the D.W.A.* My dear husband, Eamon Amun-Ra, thought my pinkies were the most delectable things he had ever tasted."

"Thank you, Mrs A. Whatever happened to your good husband?"

Mrs Amun-Ra stood and wiped her hands on her apron. "Poor Eamon, he choked to death, unfortunately."

Jim, who had just taken a large bite of one of the pinkies, locked his jaw and stopped chewing. "Really?" he asked, smiling and trying hard not to swallow.

---

* Desert Women's Association (not to be confused with the Dessert Women's Association, of which Mrs Amun-Ra was also a member).

"Yes, my goodness gracious, too right. On a twenty piastre coin, would you believe? Someone gave it to him for baksheesh and he was biting it to see if it was genuine, when – oh, but that's the way the cookie crackles, is it not? Excuse me, Mr Jim, Miss Doris, I think I spy some customers."

She reached down, tweaked Cairo Jim's cheeks, then ploughed off like a perfumed lorry.

"Here, Doris, have some pinkies." Jim moved the plate nearer to her perch and picked up his newspaper again.

"Don't mind if I do." The macaw hopped off his shoulder and down onto the table where she started to peck at one of the iced sponges.

Jim turned the newspaper's page. "Doris!" he said, almost at once. "Look who we have here."

Doris hopped back onto his shoulder, pinkie crumbs falling from her beak onto his shirt, and they both peered at the newspaper's photograph of Captain Neptune Bone. It was not a very flattering likeness, as it had been taken from below and made the dubious Captain look very much like a bearded basketball with a fez on top.

Doris read the headline above the portrait. "Raark. 'CAPTAIN BONE STILL A LARGE'." She blinked and looked at Jim. "Still a large what?"

"No, Doris, 'CAPTAIN BONE STILL AT LARGE'. You skipped the T."

"I prefer coffee," quipped the bird. When Jim didn't

 18

laugh, she quickly added, "I still reckon he's a large something or other."

"Read me what it says, my dear."

"Rightio. Ahem:

Captain Neptune F. Bone, the most unfinancial archaeologist in the Old Relics Society and noted wearer of plus-fours trousers, is wanted for questioning by the Antiquities Squad in Cairo. A spokesperson for the Squad said Bone is wanted for trying to pervert the course of archaeology, theft of photographic equipment from Miss Pyrella Frith (archaeological photographer), disruption of flabellum wafters, and for running naked through the streets of Luxor one night last September.

"Yeeergh," said Jim, screwing up his nose.

Anyone knowing the whereabouts of this suspect or his raven companion who answers to the name of Desdemona should contact Inspector Mustafa Kuppa at the Maxwell House headquarters of the Antiquities Squad. A reward will be paid handsomely.

"Hmm. I wonder where that old scallywag Bone is?"

"On another planet, I hope," said Doris. "A bigger bundle of nastiness I've *never* met." She hopped back to the plate of pinkies and clutched one up with her claw.

Jim held the newspaper in front of his face. "Nor I, my dear," he sighed. "Nor I."

Then something happened which made Jim go very quiet. His hands began to tremble and his heart was all of a sudden beating as fiercely as the surf which had sunk the *Vanderdecken* so many years before.

Cairo Jim stared at the page of the newspaper with the sun streaming down behind it and saw, because of the bright light glowing through the paper, the drawing of the Hurghada beastie on the other side of the page. What made his heart beat quicker was what he could now see on the neck of the beast.

By a curious trick of the light, Jim could not discern the horse-like head which had been drawn on top of the beast's neck; instead, superimposed by the sun, was the *pudgy, bearded, fez-topped head of Neptune Bone*!

"I'll be swoggled," Jim said softly. He went to put the newspaper down, but something stopped him. He didn't know what, but it was something to do with his imagination and his logic and his knowledge of Bone from past dealings. All of these things swirled around in his mind, flung together by the wobble of circumstance created by the glowing sunlight.

Brenda looked up. "We must go," she thought, closing her long-lashed eyelids and lowering her head so she could shut her book with her snout.

"Doris," Jim said urgently, putting down his newspaper. "We must go."

"What? Go? Go where? Raark!"

"To Hurghada." Jim rose and put on his pith helmet. "I think I know where Neptune Bone may be lurking."

"Oh, marvellous," muttered the macaw. "I need *him* like a hole in the beak!"

But Jim of Cairo did not hear her, for he was already saddling Brenda the Wonder Camel in preparation for the long journey before them.

A BEAST IN THE EAST

"BUT, JIM," FLAPPED DORIS (sitting at the front of Brenda's ornate macramé saddle as the humped dynamo galloped steadily across the sandy plains), "I don't understand."

"What don't you understand, my dear?" Jim lurched to Brenda's unchanging rhythm.

"Why you're – why *we're* going after Bone. He's such a scoundrel, such a felon! Raark. You know he is. Why, upon my crest, surely you remember how he's diddled you and swindled you and how that despicable raven tried to pluck me of every vestige of my plumage? Why on earth are we courting trouble in this way? Why are we deliberately *seeking it out*?"

"Quaaaooo," snorted Brenda, her teeth bared and the wind pulling back her nostrils.

Jim smiled at his troubled friend and tousled the feathers on her neck. "My dear Doris, we're not off on this jaunt to find Bone for the sake of finding him. Or Desdemona, for that matter. We're not off on an odyssey of hardship, no, this is a matter of truth."

"Eh?"

"Of *honour*."

"Honour?"

"Of" – and Jim's voice seemed to ride upon the wind, as though it were not the wind, but an ocean wave, and his voice was the clean, white foam at the top of it – "archaeology".

Doris blinked and looked at him in a sceptical fashion, as though he were an odd smell that had just blown around her.

"Oh, yes indeedy," nodded Jim. "We're on our way to prevent the same sort of plunder which Sir Murray Savlon dared to perpetrate so long ago. To quash the same greedy spirit which resides today inside the guts of one such as Neptune Bone. You see, Doris, a man like Bone does nothing without a motive, and in his case, the motive is always founded on colossal avarice, dishonesty and selfishness. Qualities which will always thwart the very ethos of our profession."

Jim's eyes took on a faraway dreamy quality, and he recited very quietly the Archaeological Ode he had written so many years before while he had been studying at Archaeology School:

We dig for things, we hunt and search,
we seek the lost and rusty,
those Kings and Queens left in the lurch
by History, sad and dusty.
We toil, we sweat, we cleanse our knees
with soap that makes them glisten …
we sing about Antiquities
to anyone who'll listen…

"*What?*" Doris flapped her wings in exasperation at the great amount of words her friend had said, even though (she thought) he had not said very much at all.

"Trust him," thought Brenda, as her hoofs pounded the dust, and the rising moon bathed her mane in its faint, soft glimmer.

"Trust me," said Jim, not quite knowing why.

One hundred and eighty-three kilometres away, on the flat, still waters of the Red Sea, the great Beast of Hurghada floated silently out from the shadowy, papyrus-crowded shallows.

It rode the calm mirror of the water with barely a movement, its cold beady eyes staring far off into the distance of the night, its slimy hide glinting and reflecting off the surface of the sea as straight ahead it sailed.

If you were to see the Beast from across the sand-hills you would undoubtedly stop in your tracks, startled, and a panic as heavy and as unwelcome as cold porridge or forgotten custard would grip your insides. You would gasp as you spied the Beast's horrific row of jagged teeth threshing back and forth as its cavernous mouth opened and shut. You would begin to sweat coldly behind your ears as you noticed the smoke pouring from its craterous nostrils. Then, before the porridge-like panic took hold of your nerves, you would run – as fast as you could, stumbling in the moonlight, away from this hideous freak of nature.

But only if you were to view it from such a distance, and under cover of darkness.

If you were to inspect it *close-up*, in the cold and sensible light of day, it would present a different picture. The dark, slimy skin upon its back would be nothing more than an enormous sheet of glistening rubber, dotted here and there with small, stuck-on patches, like those you put over punctures in a bicycle tyre. The cold, staring eyes would look remarkably like two lacquered tennis balls with black dots painted in the centres, and the long teeth would bear a distinct resemblance to a collection of cuttlefish shells. You would hear, as well, as it sloshed along its watery course, a most unbeastly noise: a *chugga-chugga-chugga* sound, more mechanical than monstrous.

And tonight, if you were seeing it from the eastern side (impossible unless you were a curious fish, or in a boat), you would behold a door – a rubber-covered, creaking door attached to the side of the Beast by three canvas hinges – opened wide, and a pale, honey-coloured light glimmering faintly from the creature's insides, casting a watery beam upon the glassiness below. And from the belly of the Beast, a very unmusical voice singing a dirgey song would attack your eardrums:

I'll have vast reserves of gold and jewels,
a gilt and satin chair,
oh, I just can't wait to be a billionaire. Arrr!
There'll be loads of slaves to manicure

my fingernails with care,
oh, it's fate that I should be a billionaire. Arrr!

Captain Neptune F. Bone sat in an overstuffed armchair inside what should have been the Hurghada Beast's larger intestine, but was in fact a small, hollow chamber similar to the inside of a submarine. A long cigar smoked from his fleshy lips as he buffed his fingernails with a look of sheer pleasure on his bearded face. "Arrr," he purred to himself, "if I weren't intent on being the genius archaeologist what I am, I'm certain I would have been destined for a career in the Opera."

A derisive screech came from somewhere inside the cavity within the Beast's neck, followed by a scrambling, scratching noise. Out popped the beak and blood-red eyes of Bone's raven companion, the flea-ridden Desdemona. "Craark!" spat the bird. "What as? An instant, one-man crowd?"

Bone stopped his buffing and glared up at her. "*What* did you say?" he growled.

"It wouldn't be for your voice. You sound like Maria Callas with her head stuck in a toad."

"You jealous repository of malevolence." He blew a shaft of smoke at her, which she promptly wafted with her wing up the beast's neck and towards the nostrils.

"Jealous?" Her eyes narrowed. "Me jealous of you? Nevermore!"

"What would you know of the finer things? The nearest you get to culture is when you poke your beak

into a tub of yoghurt. Or on those rare occasions when you peck the bacteria from between your claws."

The raven's eyes throbbed furiously. "At least I can see that far below," she croaked.

"*What do you mean?*"

"I *mean* that when I want to see *my* walkers I don't need to resort to a mirror. These feathers're *sleek*."

Bone looked down at his waistcoated paunch and patted it gently. "Arrr. This is success, you stupid bird. Mother always used to say, 'You can tell a successful man by his substance'."

"Successful? Craaaark! What do you mean, *successful?* Look at us, stuck out here in the middle of nowhere, you with your precious fingernails and me with no tinned seaweed to scoff. How can you call this successful?"

"Time will reveal all," Bone smirked.

Desdemona hopped down onto the rubber floor and cast him a cynical stare. "What poppycock dost thou spout?" she squawked. "Time will reveal all? What rot!"

Bone smiled a fully-in-control smile. "Think for a moment, you impetuous imbecile. Think of what we are going to accomplish. The golden sarcophagus of Pharaoh Sekheret sits resplendent somewhere far below us. When we locate it, and winch it up to the underside of our Beastie here, the immense value of it will mean that I shall never have to work for a living again. Never. Not a single, obsequious, humdrum day. I can retire from the drab world of archaeology and become what I've always wanted to become."

"A flabbier blob than you are now?"

"I'd take a swipe at you if it wouldn't rock the Beast. No, you heinous helpmeet, I would become an M.O.L."

"A *mole*? That'd be an improvement!"

"No, gormless, it's an acronym, as opposed to an acrimony, which is what you are. The letters stand for Man of Leisure."

"Oh, for the love of Zeus, now I've heard everything! I don't know why I don't just fly off and leave you to your stupendous delusions and—"

"Because you *can't*, that's why. You know as well as I, you're just as wanted as me. Inspector Mustafa Kuppa wants my guts for garters and your feathers for a duster. We cannot surface until the discovery has been made, and then we shall vamoose to somewhere isolated and tropical. I've heard that Port Moresby is nice at this time of year. While we're there, I can pick up a few more of those tailored paisley shirts that are so flattering to my greatness."

"Ratso," croaked Desdemona.

"We must lie low until Sekheret is located. People must not have an inkling of where we are, or of what we're doing. Secrecy is paramount. That's the whole reason for this elaborate vessel of artificiality." He waved his cigar around the rubber surroundings. "No one in their right mind would hang about once they'd come across such a frightful apparition. Our dear Beastie is our passport to seclusion. You see, I've thought of everything, as my natural streak of genius allows." He

took a long, smug puff on his cigar and straightened the butternut-tinted tassel on his turquoise fez.

Desdemona pecked at a flea that was making the feathers around her tarsus tingle in an unpleasant manner. She crunched it in her beak. "You live in a castle of dreams," she said scornfully. "It's only an old sarcophagus you're after. There are tons of old sarcophaguses here in Egypt, more than you could count on the fingers of the whole force of the Antiquities Squad! You'll get five hundred Egyptian pounds for it if you're lucky. Not enough to last us a week!"

"Five hundred pounds?" Bone smiled lopsidedly.

"Not a piastre more. Man of Leisure, my beak!"

"Yes, bird, for once in your pathetic life you may be right."

"You bet I'm right. Why, of all the ridiculous notions you've ever come up with, of all the outlandish—" She stopped abruptly and riveted her gaze onto Bone. "What did you just say?" she asked incredulously.

"I said you may be right."

Desdemona extended her wings behind her, propping herself against the rubber deck to save herself from fainting. "I don't believe it," she gasped. "Did I hear correctly? Did you, Neptune Flannelbottom Bone, the man who is absolutely and obstinately and *always* one hundred percent correct about *everything*, say that I may be *right*?"

"Arrr. I did, you deaf drongotoid."

"Well, I'll be a mongoose's uncle. Are you feeling

 **29**

sick or something?"

Bone locked his fingers together and cracked his knuckles loudly (Desdemona shrieked at this). "No," he smirked, "I am feeling perfectly well. It's just that what you said about the sarcophagus of Sekheret being worth only five hundred pounds is perfectly true. That *certainly* wouldn't last us a week."

"Then why, for heaven's sake, are we looking for the thing? Why all this discomfort and" – she screwed up her beak – "*rubber?*"

"I'll tell you," whispered Bone.

He lifted the starboard part of his backside and withdrew from the rear pocket of his plus-fours trousers a small, yellowed piece of newspaper. "This is a little story that appeared in *The Cairo Chronicle* on December the twenty-third, 1829," he said, unfolding the paper. "Wrap your hearing-holes around this:

MONTE CARLO, FRIDAY. Sir Murray Savlon, celebrated adventurer and gold afficionado, today broke the bank at the Monte Carlo Casino, winning four hundred and ninety-seven consecutive games of blackjack before retiring unbeaten. Casino sources estimate the total value of his winnings to be in the vicinity of sixteen million pounds. Savlon left the Casino swiftly after his win, taking with him the entire sum of his new fortune in gold doubloons.

"Craark!" squawked Desdemona.

"It continues on to say," added Bone, folding the newspaper and replacing it in his pocket, "that the authorities at the casino later discovered that Sir Murray had been cheating with five extra packs of cards concealed on his person, in a place never fully ascertained, but that's neither here nor there. Oh, *what* a success he was! Arrr."

"So what's all this got to do with us being here? With the watery coffin you're so keen to purloin?"

The extra-large man took a long puff on his foul-smelling cigar. He blew the smoke in a thick column straight at Desdemona, who quickly wafted it up the beast's neck. "Because, you demanding dustbag, I have lately come across certain information which suggests a link between Sir Murray's success on that particular occasion and the late Pharaoh's unexpected resting place."

"You mean—?"

"Arrrr," Bone giggled in a high falsetto. "I mean that Sekheret's sarcophagus contains not the subterranean sire we think. Oh, no, wily old Savlon did a bit of a switch. He switched the royal mummy for his *winnings*. The doubloons from Monte Carlo await us, sarcophagussed in all their sub-marine splendour! Aaaaaaaarrrrrrrrrrr."

Desdemona's eyes rolled up into her skull. "Sixteen million pounds?" she wheezed, and a long spittle of green slime dribbled out of her beak.

"That was in 1829," Bone whispered. "Imagine what all that magnificence would be worth today, with *inflation*."

"A topic on which you are a living, breathing, expanse of expertise."

 31

"Ha, ha. If you don't cease your insolent insinuations I shall tie and wrap you in brown paper and deposit you in a postbox, addressed to Inspector Kuppa at the Antiquities Squad in Cairo. I'm sure his tweezer hand would be *itching* to come across you."

"No way, Desiree. Craark. I'm seeing this through with you to the end!"

"Good, you domatium of docility. You know as well as I, we're in this together. For better or worse, in sickness or in stealth, for richer or richer still—"

"—for fatter or thinner?"

"Hmmph. Enough of this verbosity. Whatever is the time?" He reached down and stubbed out his cigar on the top of Desdemona's skull before pulling out his gold fob-watch from his emerald-green waistcoat.

"Aaarrrrgggghhh," shrieked Desdemona, as the glossy feathers above her forehead sizzled and singed. "Do it again! You wiped out a whole barracksful of fleas!"

"No time for pleasure, not at the moment," muttered Bone. He opened his watch and inspected the dial. "It is now ten minutes to the hour of nine. In six hundred seconds the moon will be at its highest point in the firmament, and underwater illumination will be at a maximum for night diving. Go and drop the anchor."

"Aye, aye, my Captain."

She hopped behind the armchair and pulled a lever in the tail recess. There was a *clatterclatterclatter* as the anchor on its chain dropped out from the Beast's nether regions and plunged towards the ocean floor.

"Anchor dropped, Captain Bone."

"Arrr." He closed his manicure case and stood, swaying a little as the Beast shifted under his weight. "Now help me on with the diving suit. And don't do anything into the oxygen hose again when I'm down below. Last night I nearly choked on your spitglob, you mucky mess of mange."

"You didn't like my mucus cannonball?"

"Bring me that suit!"

He donned his spatterdashes (his plus-fours were precious to him), and Desdemona dragged the black diving suit across the floor to him. For the next eight minutes he squeezed himself bit by bit, centimetre by clammy centimetre, flesh-bulge by rolling flesh-bulge, into the clinging watertight wrapping. "Arrr," he grimaced as he tugged the zipper up his oversized chest and towards his beard, "I know that when that lovely booty is mine—"

"Eh?"

"—er, *ours*, then this will all have been worth the effort."

With a grunt he secured the zip. His cheeks were scarlet and his earlobes dripped with sweat.

Desdemona said nothing, but hopped across the rubber floor to the enormous brass diving-helmet. This she nudged with her beak and pushed with her wings until it was close to Bone who, in the dim light, resembled something between a gargantuan tadpole and an over-engorged leech. He bent down, picked up the helmet with a straining grunt, lifted it over his head,

and lowered it carefully onto his round shoulders.

Desdemona followed the routine she had followed for the past fortnight and taped Bone's deluxe waterproof fez with the drip-dry tassel onto the top of the helmet. Then she attached the oxygen hose to a valve in the side of the enormous globe-like headpiece, and gave a rocketing squawk.

Neptune Bone heard the distant sound and opened the small circular door in front of his face. "Right," he rumbled. "All ready?"

"As usual," replied the raven, her eyes throbbing.

"Keep your claws crossed, birdbrain, that tonight I might harvest all my wildest desires. Arrr."

He slammed the face-door shut and (with the gait of an astronaut on the moon) clumped in his leaden boots to the door. With all of his weight on this side of the Beast, it was not surprising that the vessel rolled towards the water, and would have kept rolling, had Bone not jumped out of her.

There'll be scads of slaves to curlicue
my beard and eyebrows hair,
to wish for less it wouldn't be quite fair.
Oh, it's now that I will be a billionaire! Arrrr!

he sang inside the chamber of the helmet, but only he could hear his song.

With a splash like a small tsunami he hit the water. His helmet bobbed for several seconds amidst the

 **34**

chopping waves he had made; then he sank, the darkness of his diving suit and the darkness of his intentions bleeding out into the darkness of the Red Sea, until, with a wriggle of his considerable bottom, he was gone.

⌐⌐⌐⌐⌐ 3 ⌐⌐⌐⌐⌐

HURTLING TO HURGHADA

BECAUSE IT WAS SUCH a long way from Gurna to Hurghada, Jim, Doris and Brenda had never expected to make the trip in one uninterrupted go. They had stopped galloping very late in the night – very near to midnight, to be precise – and had camped out, under the stars, at a small but sheltered oasis they had, by chance, discovered.

At five o'clock the next morning Doris gave an ear-shattering screech very close to Jim's sleeping head. "*Raaaaarrrrrrrkakakakakaraaaarrrk!*"

Cairo Jim sprang bolt upright, his eyes as wide as saucers. By the edge of the small lagoon, Brenda, too, awoke with a snorting start.

"Jim, Jim," squawked the macaw, "you'll never guess what I just dreamt!"

"What – what time is it?" Squinting, the archaeologist-poet felt around in the sand for his desert sun-spectacles.

"I had this extra-*or*dinary dream that I was in the most splendiferous stationery shop! There I was, the only one present, surrounded by shelves piled high, all the way to the ceiling, with pencils and erasers and sharpeners and fountain pens and bottles of ink and coloured paper and wooden rulers and lots of little

 **36**

knobbly rubber things, like that woman at the post office—"

"Quaaaooo?" snorted Brenda, who had never been allowed into the post office (which to her was an Everlasting Mystery), and had always been curious about the woman who worked inside it.

"Let me finish, Brenda," flapped Doris. "Just like that woman at the post office *wears on her thumb* when she's counting out stamps. Well, there I am, rark, minding my own feathers and just gawking with my beak open at all this mountain of stationery, when who do you think walks into the shop?"

"Goodness, Doris, I really don't know. Now, where did I put those—"

"Hamlet, Prince of Denmark, of course. The man himself. No more, no less. In he comes, all dressed in black – as is his preference, don't you know – and he's looking all sort of morose and glum – which isn't terribly surprising considering he's Hamlet, Prince of Denmark, and that's how he usually looks – but today, in this stationery shop, he's looking even moroser and glummer than usual. So I fly over to him and say, 'Greetings, salutations, oh Hamlet, Prince of Denmark. Prithee, why the royal sourpuss?' And do you know what he says?"

"Maybe they're in my pocket."

"No, no, rark, he says, 'Oh brave and learned macaw Doris, late of Peru and now of Egypt, I am most distressed. I have, forsooth, lost my pencil.' 'Oh?' says I, in a respectful but concerned manner, as befits the way

you would address Hamlet, Prince of Denmark, when he's fretting in a well-stocked stationery shop. 'And what, oh, noble Prince, what sort of pencil was it?' And do you know what he answered?"

"I have no idea," said Jim, patting the pockets in his extra-wide shorts.

"'2B or not 2B, that is the question.' Ha, ha, ha, ha, ha, reeeerraaarrk!"

She hopped up and down, flapping her wings gleefully, until suddenly there was a dull thunking sound, and her beak thwaaaaaaanged up into her face. "Jmm, Jmm," she grunted, "t's hppnd gn. Gt bt xctd. Hlp m pls?"

"Certainly, my dear." He reached down and gently, but with just the right amount of force, reset her mandible.

"That's better," she said, moving it back and forth.

Brenda, by now on her hoofs and completely puzzled by Doris's dream and the effect it had had on the excitable macaw, lumbered over to Jim and nuzzled him softly in the centre of his back. "Quaaoo."

"What's that, my lovely?" He turned to her and his face broke out in a huge grin. "Well, hang coconuts from my ears and call me a palm tree! Doris, Doris, look at what Brenda's found."

He reached to her mouth and removed his pair of desert sun-spectacles which she had been holding tenderly between her jaws. "Thank you, you Wonderful thing."

Brenda snorted and fluttered her eyelashes.

"Reerk," said Doris, moving her neck up and down and hopping about on one claw. "Are we going to stand around here all day *admiring* one another, or go after Bone?"

Jim strapped on his pith helmet and threw Brenda's saddle over her humps. He fastened it underneath her belly and hoisted himself up onto her back, extending his arm in Doris's direction when he had made himself comfortable. "You're right, my dear. Hop on and we'll be off."

"And not before time," Doris squawked in a bossy tone. She gave a few flaps of her huge wings and, before you could say "Sekheret", she was on Jim's arm, and the intrepid trio were but a cloud of sandy dust rising above the oasis.

They travelled earnestly, steadfastly, perspiringly, across sand dunes as tall as skyscrapers, past withered oases and the remains of ancient temples that had been levelled by time and neglect into lines of flat and crumbling foundation stones. The sun rose like a blister in the skies, and soon the whole landscape in front of them was barely visible through a shimmering haze of frizzy heat.

"Talk about hot," gasped Jim in between mouthfuls of water from his water-bottle.

"All right," said Doris, "if you want me to. 'Fie! This is hot weather, gentlemen,' as Mr Shakespeare wrote in *Henry the Fourth Part Two* – Act Three, Scene Two, if you

want to know. Rark. As we are all aware, the hotness of the day is a necessary thing for the formation and continuation of all types of life upon the planet Earth. If it were not hot, we would probably have another Ice Age, just like the one that destroyed the dinosaur race so long ago. Heat is vital—"

"No, Doris," interrupted Jim. "It was only a figure of speech."

"Quaaaooo," Brenda snorted hotly.

At five minutes after two in the afternoon, Brenda approached an old wooden sign that had become burned and faded by the sun. She immediately stopped galloping and slowed to a steady, inquisitive, lumbering pace. Cairo Jim took his binoculars from her saddle-bag and focussed on the sign's letters.

"What's it say?" blinked Doris.

"At last," smiled Jim. "It says:

YOU ARE NOW APPROACHING HURGHADA
KEEP GOING OVER THE HILL.
THE ONE YOU'RE CLIMBING NOW.
JUST A LITTLE MORE.
NO FISHING NO HUNTING NO DOGS
NO NO NO NANETTE.

"Wacko," said Doris. She flapped her wings and ascended from Brenda's rear hump, flying off a little distance ahead of them.

Jim leaned close to Brenda's ear. "Come on, my lovely," he whispered, "we're not going to let her beat us, are we?"

Brenda snorted and her mane bristled with competitiveness. She picked up her hooves and sped off after the flighty macaw.

Up the small sandhill Brenda galloped, Jim gripping her saddle tightly with his knees, until she stood at the top, her coat glistening and her eyelashes quivering with pleasure.

Doris circled in the sky above them, giving short, sharp screeches of exhilaration. When Jim looked ahead, he could see why.

Before them the sand came to an abrupt end, and the enormous blue sparkle of the Red Sea spread out in all its watery glory. Small crests of white foam glinted like mirrors catching the sun's rays, and a cool, refreshing breeze whirled and sped across the surface of the water and up to Jim, Doris and Brenda, ruffling the Wonder Camel's mane and puffing up Jim's shorts and down his clinging shirt.

"Anyone fancy a dip?" screeched Doris, diving down through the air to the water. Just as it appeared that she was going to disappear beak-first beneath the surface, she tacked sharply to the left and shot speedily in a line parallel to the sea, her wing tips skimming the white crests of foam.

"What a good idea," said Jim, to which Brenda snorted agreeably.

 **41**

He sprang down, unbuckled her saddle and bridle, hauled them away, and off she trotted towards the coolness ahead. As she tested the water temperature with her hoof, Jim tore off his shirt, pith helmet, desert sun-spectacles, boots and socks, and ran to join her.

"Come on, you two!" cried Doris, still flitting close to the water (but not getting more than a few feathers wet). "The world might end at any moment!"

"Last one in's a rotten scarab," Jim shouted to Brenda, but before he had sounded the final "b" in "scarab", the Wonder Camel had run and plunged underwater. In an instant, her head and front hump emerged and she snorted at him as she would have at a rotten scarab.

Jim laughed and threw himself in, too.

Doris flapped down to land on Brenda's above-water hump and, for a few minutes, rode Brenda as she paddled around. The bird ordered Brenda about all the while, as though she were a ship and Doris the skipper.

"Look out for rocks, raark, mind that wave there, watch for snags, steady on, Brenda, too fast, too fast!"

This all became too much for Brenda, who, without any warning, submerged her entire body. "Reerarrk," Doris squawked, shooting upwards before she got a bellyful of Red Sea.

Cairo Jim thought this was all very funny.

For twenty minutes they splashed and swam and wallowed and let the small waves roll over them. Then their frolics were interrupted by a sound that, even

beneath the water, made Jim's blood run cold.

"*Aaaawwwuuuuuuuggggh!*"

Brenda stopped paddling and Doris stopped splashing.

"What – what was that?" whispered Jim. They listened for the sound to come again. Several moments passed, but all they heard was the rise and fall of the coastal wind and the soft lapping of the waves against their body and humps and wing tips.

Then it returned.

"*Aaaawwwwwwuuuuuuuuugggggggh!*" This time louder and more woeful than before. It was the sort of sound that made skin, hair and feathers prickle, then stomachs tingle, then coldness spread across the back of one's neck as if someone had just cracked a chilled egg there. And all of that in three seconds flat.

"It's the most awful, most pitiful moan I've ever heard," said Jim. "Is it human?"

"No," said Doris, her head cocked to the north. "No, it is not the sound of a human being. It is an ornithological exclamation of loss and misery."

"Yes?" Jim said.

"Quaaaooo?"

"AAAAWWWWUUUUUUUUUUUUGGGGGGGGGH!" came the sound, this time so loudly it seemed to echo all the way down to the Valley of the Kings and back again. Brenda shuddered in the water.

The feathers on Doris's brow creased. "That sound," she informed them gravely, "is the loneliest sound in the whole of the Bird Realm. I have only ever heard it once

 **43**

before, when I was quite a young macaw, but I could never forget the sheer hollowness of it."

"What *is* it?" implored Jim.

"It is – the Lamentation of the Raven!"

Cairo Jim gasped as he realised what that meant. Quickly he began to swim back to shore. "Come on, gang," he called over his shoulder between strokes. "Where there's a wail, there's a way."

"To what?" called Doris.

"To Neptune Bone!"

ᘒᘱᗑᘐᗐ **4** ᘒᘱᗑᘐᗐ

LAMENTATION OF A RAVEN

THEY DRIED THEMSELVES as quickly as they could, and donned clothes and saddle. In no time at all they were patrolling the shoreline, their ears and hearing-holes open and alert for the gruesome noise.

Up and down the sand Brenda crept. Jim, riding warily on her saddle, had taken out his binoculars and was scanning the sandhills to the north, while Doris kept an earnest watch from the crown of his pith helmet.

The breeze died away to not even a flyblow, and the air was strangely, *threateningly*, still.

Brenda continued to skirt the water's edge, the hairs in her mane bristling with concentration. All at once she gave a terrific snort and reared up onto her hind legs. "Quaaaaoooo!"

Jim gripped her bridle tightly, and Doris scrambled atop his hat, her wings blurring as she tried to maintain her balance.

"Raark! What is it, Brenda?"

The Wonder Camel reared again, the sand flying from her hoofs.

"Look, Doris, over there beyond that bend. Steady on, Brenda my lovely, it won't hurt you."

 **45**

"Quaaaaoooo," protested Brenda, but this time she did not rear.

Jim reached forward and stroked the side of her massive neck. "It's all right," he soothed. "You and Doris stay here. I'll go and check it out."

Before either Brenda or Doris had a moment to protest, Jim had leapt down (Doris fluttering onto Brenda's empty saddle), removed his umbrella from Brenda's saddlebag, and thus armed, was advancing towards the hostile-looking, glaring head which was emerging above the sandhill in front of them.

Jim's walk was neither confident nor tentative as he approached the repulsive cranium. It was more a *cranky* walk (with a little bit of fear thrown in as well) – he was irate that something had upset Brenda so much.

Now he began to get curious, for the closer he came to it, the more the hardened eyes seemed to glaze over, and the more frozen the visage seemed to become. The jagged teeth were losing their ferociousness, and the creature's slimy hide was, before Jim's very eyes, transforming into a huge expanse of taut, patched rubber.

Jim lowered his umbrella, letting the tip rest in the sand. "It's all right, gang," he called, "it's only a pile of tennis balls and cuttle shells and mended rubber that's beached on the shore. The Beast is bogus, just like I'd—"

"*Aaaaawwwwwwwuuuuuuuuuuuuuuuggggggggh!*" came the agonised cry, so close to the archaeologist that he dropped his umbrella and turned to race back to Doris and Brenda.

Only he didn't.

His eye, as he was about to sprint off, had caught on a limp, glossy bundle of feathers which lay tangled upon the sand. Jim blinked, and squinted behind his sun-spectacles, and realised what it was: the raven Desdemona, lying on her pot-belly with her head buried under her wings.

Turning to Doris and Brenda, Jim gestured for them to join him. They came quickly and saw the raven, whose posture Brenda recognised immediately (from certain scenes in old, silent movies) as being one of Stricken Grief. She gave a piteous snort. "Quaaao?"

The noise came like gunfire to the raven's hearing-holes, and in a flash of fleas and feathers and sand she rolled over onto her back, sprang onto her claws, and held her tatty wings wide open. "Captain?" she croaked, blinking her watery, red eyes.

"Desdemona?" said Jim.

The raven's eyes narrowed as she saw the trio before her. "*Bleccch!*" She spat a few grains of sand into the wind. "It's only you lot. What are you doing here? Is the Archaeological Kindergarten on holidays or something?"

Doris fluttered up onto Jim's shoulder, her feathers bristling indignantly.

Jim chose to ignore the intended insult. "I might well ask that question of you," he said. "The middle of nowhere by the Red Sea seems a strange place for a bird the likes of you, and a creature the likes of that" – he looked across at the Beast – "and, presumably, an archaeologist the likes of *Neptune Bone*."

At the sound of her companion's name, Desdemona threw herself once again into a heap on the sand and, opening her beak as wide as it could go, let forth her Lamentation:

"AAAAWWWWUUUUUUUUUUUGGGGGGGGGH!"

Brenda made her ears flap down to shut out the sound, and Doris's plumage stood on end.

"My goodness," Jim said to the macaw, "I think something's happened to Bone'.

"Eh?" said Doris.

"Yes." Jim frowned. "The way she reacted to the sound of his name. I'd say something's definitely not right."

Desdemona stopped her wailing and now, her tongue hanging dribblingly out of her opened beak, she glared at them with glazed, bloodshot pupils. "You bet your obelisks something's not right," she rasped. "Oh, why? Why, why, why? How could the gods be so ca-r*uel*?" And she did another Lamentation, as shudderingly piercing as all the rest.

Jim waited patiently until she had finished. Then he asked, in a worried voice, "Where *is* Captain Bone?"

This time at the mention of his name, Desdemona did not go hurtling into paroxysms of gloom. Instead, she narrowed her eyes to thin, hatchet-like slits, and began to mutter, like an out-of-control gramophone whose speed is being fiddled with:

"Don't know how it could've happened. He'd done that dive every night for a fortnight, it's not as though it was a first. Down, down, down, down, down to the

depths of despair." She broke off to savagely peck at a flea on her hip, then raised her head and held her wings high. "Accursed be the name of Sekheret!" she proclaimed.

"Sekheret?" whispered Jim, and Doris's crest plumage arched forward. "He was diving for Sek—?"

"Diving for Sir Murray Savlon's deposits," spat the raven.

"So that's what the Beast is for?" asked Jim.

It was his idea, not mine. He said it would scare people off and leave us to do our findings in peace. Dratted doubloons! Oh, I know we never really got on that well, I know we were both exiles thrung together by the harsh, cold tentacle of the Law, but" – and her slitty eyes became wide and glistening – "he was my *friend*. Hoo hoo hoo!"

"Desdemona! Where is he?"

"Dead," she wailed. "Nevermore, nevermore, nevermore. Dead, dead, dead, and never called me Dessie!"

Cairo Jim sucked his breath in sharply. "What? Neptune Bone, *dead*? Are you quite certain?"

"He never came up again," she answered gravely. "The flab has floundered, the skunk has sunk, the heinous genius has died by his schemius. Bone got the bends! He's been shishkebabbed by sharks! Cancelled out by calamari! Polished off by perch, eradicated by eels, wiped out by whales, put away by porpoises, carted off by clams, obliterated by octopi, abolished by

abalones! He's been done in by the deep. Hoo hoo hoo."

"Neptune Bone, *dead*?" muttered Jim, shaking his head. "I can hardly begin to believe it—"

"Oh, it's true all right," blubbed Desdemona, her voice almost choking in her oesophagus. "Work it out for yourself. He's been down there all night with no oxygen!"

"No oxygen?"

The raven grunted and hopped across to the open door in the Beast's hide. She poked her head in, rummaged around for a moment, and pulled out the oxygen hose. With this clenched in her beak she hopped quickly over to Jim's feet and dropped it in the sand. "That's what came up after an hour," she croaked. "Look at the end of it."

Jim reached down (Doris holding onto his shoulder tightly) and picked up the section of black hose. He lifted his sun-spectacles and peered at it carefully. "For the love of Ozymandias," he whispered. "Look, Doris, look at these marks."

Doris squinted. "Raark. Bite marks?"

"It's as though this has been dragged from his mouth, and he didn't let go without a fight."

"*Wrenched*, I'd say," rasped Desdemona. "Something wrenched it out. There was a kerfuffle down there, or I'm not malignant."

Jim ran the hose through his hands. "Whatever could have happened? I never thought Neptune Bone would come to such an – unnoticeable end. I always thought

he'd go out with all blunderbusses blazing, with everyone aware that we were losing a figure of his self-proclaimed stature. Goodness, I suppose I thought he'd issue a press release about it or something."

"There's another thing." Desdemona hopped back to the Beast and extricated a small, squat object. She brought this back to Jim, Doris and Brenda, and lovingly, tenderly, placed it on the sand. "It's his deluxe waterproof fez with the drip-dry tassel. He thieved – bought it especially for this venture. Used to make me sticky-tape it to the top of his diving helmet before he'd go down." The upper edge of her beak was trembling. "Have a look inside," she instructed, turning her head away.

Jim picked it up and inverted it. Inside, scrawled around the crown, was something quite unexpected.

"Read it out aloud," Desdemona said, closing her throbbing eyes.

Jim licked his dry lips and read in a quiet, uncertain tone: "'whoever finds this, send help quickly – am besieged from all sides – being carted off – is this at'."

There Jim stopped, because, apart from a gaudy identification tag bearing the name CAPTAIN NEPTUNE F. BONE B.AR stuck inside the rim, there was no more writing.

"He must've scribbled it with that waterproof crayon he always carried," scowled Desdemona.

"'Is this at'," repeated Jim. "Whatever did he mean?"

"Maybe he was going to write 'is this at the end?'" suggested Doris.

 **51**

Jim frowned.

"Or maybe," squawked Desdemona, "he was going to write something about his fez, only he called it his hat without the aitch? 'Is this 'at complimentary to the colour of my eyes?'" She sighed. "He always *was* very fashion-conscious, right up to the end."

"Or maybe," said Jim, "he was writing 'is this *attack*?' and he didn't finish it?"

At about that moment, Brenda (who had been listening attentively to all of this) happened to glimpse, a few metres out from the shore, a single bubble, no bigger than a ping-pong ball, rising slowly up underneath the water. It hit the flat surface and exploded silently, leaving barely a ripple, unseen by all except her.

She raised her head and snorted into the air. Jim looked over at her and made contact with her big eyes. A thought began spiralling down from his brain, down through his neck, all the way into the space between his lungs, the place where his optimism resided. The thought shot into his optimism chamber and shot out again and, even more lightning-like than before, it zinged back along the fore-travelled route to his brain.

"Wait!" he exclaimed. "Suppose Bone's *not* dead!"

Doris blinked. "What? Are you barmy?"

"Suppose he's still down there, alive and – trapped?"

"What poppycock dost thou spout?" Desdemona spat. "It's impossible! He's been down too long."

"But *where* is he?" Jim began to pace the sand. "We

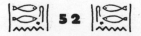

have no conclusive evidence that he's actually drowned, have we? A deluxe waterproof fez with drip-dry tassel and a messy message scrawled in it doesn't automatically mean that he's backstroked off into the After Life, does it? We shouldn't give up just yet. Maybe he's taken shelter somewhere? Maybe he's – maybe he's found the sarcophagus of Sekheret and has ensconced himself inside it so that a pack of sharks can't get at him? Maybe—"

But he trailed off, for the idea behind what he was about to utter was too wild and imaginative even for *him*.

"All righty, you cloud-headed, pith-helmeted fool," squawked Desdemona derisively. "Suppose he's still down there, breathing and gurgling away and filing his fingernails? *How do we get to him?*"

Doris gulped at the thought of all that water.

"We go to Cairo," Jim answered.

"*What?*" Desdemona shrieked.

"To the Old Relics Society. My friend and patron, Gerald Perry Esquire, has often mentioned an elderly gentleman who many years ago pioneered marvellous inventions in the area of marine archaeology. We'll look this man up and see what he has to suggest to equip us for the dive. Then we'll come back here and try to find Bone."

"It'll take too long," spat the raven. "If Bone hasn't fluffed it *yet*, he will have by the time you get back."

"Brenda will ride like the wind, won't you, my lovely?"

"Quaaaooo!"

"And anyway, that's a chance we'll have to take," flapped Doris.

"Why can't you go down now?"

"Because," Jim explained to the impatient, flea-festered one, "it's probably twenty fathoms deep. I've no equipment to withstand the pressure of the water that far down. We'll need aqualungs and special suits and all kinds of thingummies."

"Well what if, when you do get down there, the Captain is nevermore?" The raven sounded fearful.

"Then," said Jim solemnly, "we'll have done our best and will have treated the memory of a fellow archaeologist, no matter how underhanded and devious he might have been, with respect. He was not always an adverse type of man, at least not when he entered our profession."

Jim handed the deluxe waterproof fez with the drip-dry tassel back to Desdemona. "Would you care to come to Cairo with us?" he asked.

"No, no, by the poet Poe. I must stay here and keep vigil."

Brenda lumbered over and Jim hoisted himself onto her saddle. "Good idea," he said, strapping his pith helmet under his chin.

Doris fluttered from his shoulder and perched on the leather knob at the rear of the saddle. "Raark, yes, you never know what might happen."

"Promise me one thing, Cairo Jim," crarked the raven.

"What?"

"That if you come across that Inspector Mustafa Kuppa, you won't tell him where we are? I mean, where I *am* and Bone *was*? Or *is*? Oh, this is all so confusing—"

"I won't tell hint of the whereabouts of Bone," replied Jim, "because I'm not sure myself. And if you know what's good for you, you'll keep your beak low and stop doing your Lamentations so loudly."

"I'll stop for good," Desdemona squawked. "There's a queue of migraines in my skull already."

Jim turned Brenda towards the sandhills that led to the road that led to Cairo. "We'll be as quick as time allows," he called as the trio galloped off.

"Be quicker than that," Desdemona rasped in the sandstream billowing from the wake of their trail, "if there is to be any hope at all."

TO THE OLD RELICS SOCIETY

BRENDA DID INDEED RIDE like the wind; a wind with a thousand fire-crackers behind it.

She covered distances previously uncovered by even a Wonder Camel in such record time, and through all the galloping and sand flying in the breeze, Cairo Jim kept thinking about Bone and wondering what fate had befallen him. Still the kernel of belief that Bone may be alive rattled inside his body.

With the repetitive rhythm of Brenda's hoofbeats, these thoughts and this belief travelled to the poetry cells in Jim's brain, and before he was aware, a poem had formed. With no warning to Doris (who usually preferred one) or Brenda, he recited it aloud, as the scenery flashed past:

He'll lust for gold, he'll bust for gold, he'll live solely and *just* for gold,
he craves it like some others caviar.
He worships all its power,
he'd bathe in its lustrous shower,
if only he could liquefy it. Ha!
This lust for gold, this must for gold, this passion for the *dust* of gold

has manifested into his sad notion
that wealth can be obtained
via Pharaoh's casket gained
from its resting place at bottom of the ocean.
This lust for gold, this thrust for gold, the wind that
blows the *gust* of gold
has buffeted old Bone with an ill breeze.
Now who knows where he's diving,
or malingering, or conniving,
who knows what trembles lurk about his knees?

When he had finished his recitation he smiled a grim-set smile, and stared ahead as the suburbs of Cairo started to come into view.

Doris (who had forced herself, out of loyalty and with gritted beak, to listen to this newest piece of verse) roiled her eyes up into her head and urged Brenda to go faster, by slapping her firmly on the rump with her wing.

With great agility and sure-hoofed nerve, Brenda wove in and out of the bustle of Cairo's motorcars, horse-drawn carts, goat herds and darting pedestrians, until she entered Tahrir Square.

Twenty minutes later, at the end of Talaat Harb Street, the gleaming cream-coloured granite pillars outside the Old Relics Society glinted like trunks of shining palm trees.

Doris squawked excitedly. "Reeraark! Almost there. Come on, Brenda, mount them steps!"

The Wonder Camel found a final spurt of energy and bolted through the traffic, oblivious to the cacophony of horns and the shouting of motorists and the screeching of excitable Tanganyikan flamingos, who for some reason had decided to congregate in the centre of the road. She reached the stairs and, without missing a beat, bounded swiftly up them, darted between the creamy pillars, and shot through the opened doors and into the vestibule with its floor of white marble and porphyry. Here she came to a skidding halt at the large reception bureau.

At the sound of Brenda's hoofs squealing on the slippery floor, the man at the bureau looked up quickly. "Oh," he said, in rather an unsurprised voice when he saw who had arrived. "Cairo Jim. How good to see you again, away from the field. Welcome back."

"Thank you, Spong." Jim removed his pith helmet and wiped his forehead. "Is Gerald Perry around?"

"Oh, yes indeed. He and that Mr Horneplush have been in the clubroom for the past three days. Neither of them have budged from there."

"Whatever are they doing?"

"Having a staring contest," answered Spong.

"What?"

"They're just sitting there, opposite each other, looking at each other's eyes."

"Without blinking?"

"Oh, they're blinking, all right, but that's about it. The rest of the time one set of eyeballs is fixed firmly on

the other, and won't move a millimetre. It's like a scene from a movie where the film's got stuck in the projector. No movement at all, apart from the blinking."

"How very strange," said Jim.

"We think it's some sort of wager," Spong whispered confidentially. "There's something riding on it, I'm sure."

"Rark," squawked Doris impatiently. "And we're riding on Brenda, who's almost dead on her feet. The clubroom, you say?"

"Yes, indeed," nodded Spong.

"Come on, Brenda," Doris commanded, flapping her wing gently against Brenda's haunches.

"Thank you, Spong," called Jim as they trotted away down the corridor.

The doors to the clubroom were shut, so Jim quietly dismounted and took hold of Brenda's bridle. Then he gently opened one of the doors and the trio entered the dim, cedar-panelled room.

The place was almost empty, so it didn't take long to find Perry and Horneplush. There they were, both of them ensconced in their favourite armchairs by one of the tall windows. Just as Spong had said, their gazes were indeed fixed intently upon each other's.

Jim led Brenda and Doris to the centre of the room, and stopped by one of the fat and ponderous chess sets. "Stay here for a moment, my friends," he whispered. "This might be like waking sleepwalkers – I don't know how they're going to react."

"Rightio," prowked Doris, and Brenda fluttered her eyelashes.

On the tips of his Sahara Boots, Jim crept over to the gentlemen, until he was standing directly behind Esmond Horneplush's chair, across from Gerald Perry. Perry had not even noticed Jim's figure appearing in his sphere of vision; his eyes remained steadily and, it seemed to Jim, *defiantly* glued to his companion's. The clubroom was as quiet as a butterfly's whisper. The two men could have been waxwork dummies.

Then Jim spoke.

"Perry? It's me, Jim. Anyone at home?"

What happened next happened so quickly that if *you* had blinked you would have missed it: Gerald Perry looked up at Jim with such a jolt he might have just been jabbed in the bottom by a pygmy's sharpened dart, and Esmond Horneplush leapt to his feet – the top of his head narrowly missing Jim's chin – and rushed decrepitly towards the door, waving his hands in the air and shouting very excitedly about flabellums. "The breeze is mine," he sang, as he disappeared into the corridor.

"Oh, Jim," said Perry, rising to shake his hand. "Oh, what a shame."

"I hope we haven't come at an inopportune moment," said Jim, sensing the disappointment in Perry's voice.

"Eh? Oh, hello, Doris, Brenda. Oh, no, of course not." Perry's possum-like eyes instantly took on their old sparkle again. "I'd grown tired of all of that by

yesterday afternoon, if you want to know the truth."

"What was it?"

"A bet old Esmond made."

"A bet?"

"Mm-hm. The flabellum wafters have gone on strike again – you know, those three, tall, silent men who waft the flabellums in here – and Horneplush threw down the gauntlet that whoever out of the two of us broke the stare first would have to waft a flabellum over the other one until the real flabellum wafters came back on the job. Guess who lost?"

"Oh, I'm sorry, Perry."

"No bother, my friend. I'll just hide in the bathroom whenever he wants me to waft it. Now, tell me, what brings you up to see us? Not another poem you want published in the Society's newsletter, is it?"

"No—"

"Good-o," said Perry with relief.

"—it's a matter of grave urgency," answered Jim.

Perry sat down, and invited Jim to do likewise. "I'm listening, Jim. Tell me all."

As speedily and as clearly as he could, the archaeologist-poet did so. Perry listened attentively, running his thumbnail around the edges of his small moustache, and nodding slowly at various points in the tale.

When Jim had finished, Perry said, "But Jim, do you really think Bone might still be alive?"

"I don't know," answered Jim. "Maybe I'm being

hopeful, but there are things about it all that don't quite make sense. The way there were bite marks on Bone's oxygen hose, as though it'd been wrenched out, and the deluxe waterproof fez with the drip-dry tassel, for instance. He had time to scrawl the message inside the fez, to ask for help to be sent. If he were being attacked by some predator, say, *how* would he have had the time to request help? A shark would have polished him off quick-smart. And he wrote that he was besieged from all sides, and being carted off. Carted off by *what*? Something's fishy about it all, no pun intended."

"No pun taken," muttered the old gentleman gravely.

"That last bit has really got me wondering: 'is this at'. How bamboozling."

"Maybe," said Perry, "he was going to write 'is this attractive handwriting?' I wouldn't put it past the vainglorious man."

Cairo Jim shook his head.

"Tell me this," Perry frowned. "Why ever was Neptune Bone diving? He can't have been doing it for pleasure, surely? What was he after?"

"Sekheret?" suggested Jim.

"Eh, oh, goodness, no. Gave 'em up long ago. Filthy habit, made m'teeth go all—"

"No, Gerald, *Pharaoh* Sekheret. Don't you remember?"

Perry's mouth fell open. "Of course," he gasped. "The sunken King. That Savlon disaster. I'd quite forgotten! I'm almost ashamed of m'self to say so. Oh,

it's been such a long time since anyone around here has even breathed Sekheret's name, let alone *searched* for him. It's as though he's faded off into the mists of obscurity. Unremembered by everyone. That rotten Murray Savlon, why, if I'd been around in *his* day, I'd have taken to him with a wet—"

"Maybe *not* unremembered by everyone," interrupted Jim. Perry looked at him with twinkling eyes. "Do you remember how occasionally you've told me about a man – a clever archaeologist of another generation – who pioneered great breakthroughs in underwater archaeology?"

"Mm? Why, yes, old *Teddy*. Oh, he was clever, no doubt about it. Some felt he was *too* clever for his own good, and it eventually drove him a bit strange."

"Strange?"

"No one took any notice of what he was doing, you see. There he was, coming up with these magnificent ideas for aquatic exploration and marine dating of submerged artefacts, the most original and exciting notions, positively brilliant, and the people who could have helped him – the people who could have funded his explorations and theories and experiments – chose to ignore it all. A torment of frustration! It certainly took its toll on the poor chap. Made him go and become a recluse, shut away all the time with his ideas and his dreams. I wish *Horneplush*'d become a recluse sometimes, especially when it comes to *flabellums*. Yes, old Teddy, poor chap. I prefer to think that he was *ahead of his time*." Perry clasped

his hands in the lap of his white linen trousers and made a tch–tch–tch sound.

"What ever happened to old Teddy?" Jim asked urgently. "Is it possible that he's still alive?"

"Eh? Oh, yes, certainly is. At least he was the last time we saw him."

"When was that?"

"Ooh – must be getting on five years ago now."

Jim gulped. "I was hoping that, if old Teddy is still alive and if we can find him, he might be able to help us find Bone. A fellow archaeologist is caught in a sticky situation, and I think we should do our utmost."

"Well, there's one easy way to find out."

"How?" Jim could feel his hands becoming moist, and he couldn't help thinking that it was probably nothing compared to how moist Neptune Bone's hands probably were at the moment.

"We'll go down and pay old Teddy a visit. He's just downstairs, you know."

Jim turned to Doris and Brenda. "Did you hear that, my dears?"

"Rark! Too right!"

"Quaaoo!"

Perry stood and began shuffling towards the door. "It'll give me a chance to get out of here before old Horneplush comes back. I waft for no man."

"Where exactly downstairs *is* Teddy?" asked Jim, walking after him and leading Brenda by the bridle.

"In one of the Ponder Rooms."

"Ponder Rooms?"

"Ah, yes," smiled Perry. "You're a bit young to know about them yet, aren't you? It's where the more elderly archaeologists and excavationists go when they want to begin their ponderings. Either there, or to the Pontification Rooms, depends on their temperaments, really. Then they usually end up in one of the Memoirs Rooms."

"Where they write their—"

"Exactly."

Perry led them through the corridor, then into another, then another. At the end of this they descended a long flight of burgundy-coloured marble stairs which took them far down beneath the ground floor of the Society headquarters.

"Rerark," chirped Doris. "It's cool down here, all right."

"It certainly is, my dear," said Jim. "One question, Perry: what's Teddy's last name?"

Gerald Perry had to think for a moment. "Snorkel!" he finally answered. "Yes, that's it. Of course, Snorkel's not his *real* name, that's *Frobes* if I remember rightly, but Frobes never suited old Teddy, not really. So one day somebody called him *Snorkel*, on account of his predilections, and Snorkel stuck."

They walked on, their shoes and hoofs echoing on the marble floor.

"Now, let's see – ah, yes, we go round here. Funny how some names don't fit their owners, isn't it? I went

to school once with a boy called Gaunt – his last name, that is – and he was anything *but* gaunt. Ooh, whenever he jumped into the swimming pool— Oh, look, here we are, Teddy's door's down there."

They approached a large wooden door at the far end of a corridor lined with identical doors. On this particular door there was no number, or sign, or anything which made it look different to any of the others. Perry turned to Jim, Doris and Brenda and gave them a wink.

"He's very old, you know," he told them in a whisper. "But I think he'll be glad to see you."

Jim's heart was beating loudly, Doris's feathers were tingling, Brenda's humps felt like they had gone hollow. Perry raised his hand and knocked politely on the door; then they waited patiently for a response from within.

THE INNER SANCTUM OF
TEDDY SNORKEL

FOR ALMOST A FULL MINUTE they heard nothing
– the silence was heavy enough to mock the very air
containing it. Gerald Perry Esquire looked at Jim, Jim at
Doris, and Doris at Brenda. Brenda looked at her hoofs.
Then Perry tried again, his fist trembling as it made
contact with the wooden door.

The sound of the knock echoed through the door
and into whatever lay on the other side. Once again,
there was nought but quiet to greet it.

"Oh, dear," whispered Perry. "It doesn't seem as
though there's—"

"Maybe we should—" whispered Jim.

"Coo," whispered Doris.

Brenda fluttered her eyelashes, letting the coolness
soak in.

"*Entah*!" came a voice from the other side. Jim felt his
heart jump against his ribs. Doris blinked, and her beak
creased around the edges. Brenda opened her eyes wide.

"Well, knock me down with a mongoose," said Gerald
Perry. "Come on, then, let's not keep him waiting."

"Certainly not," said Jim, becoming eagerer by the
minute.

Perry gripped the doorknob and slowly turned it. He gingerly pushed the heavy door open, and the foursome stepped inside.

They entered a middle-sized room, dimly lit by a high candelabra which had four short candles burning on it. The room was sparsely decorated: the walls were bare, and painted in a pleasing apricot colour, and there was a single Persian rug on the floor in the centre of the space. On the rug was a small table, covered by a plain green silk cloth. Upon the cloth was a round fish bowl, inside which was a single goldfish, swimming around in lazy circles. Its surroundings were just as sparse as that of the room.

Opposite the fish bowl was a tall rocking-chair, and sitting in this was a small, wizened man with a mass of thick tangly silver hair, tiny round spectacles covering his flat, grey eyes, and what some would call a rather generous nose. He peered through the dimness at his visitors.

"Hello, Teddy." Perry advanced with his hand extended, and the small man stood.

"Oh," he said in a tone which clearly indicated he had not expected callers. "Why, if it isn't Marjorie."

"Er, it's not actually," said Perry.

"Are you sure?" asked Teddy Snorkel, inspecting him wistfully. "You *look* like Marjorie Wutherspoon."

"No, no, it's me. Gerald Perry."

Teddy Snorkel stepped back, and looked Perry up and down, frowning. He took off his spectacles and

repeated the procedure. "Oh, yes," he said at last. "Perry! Howdja do." They shook hands. "You must forgive me, I've been looking at the fish for so long, and *it* reminds me very much of Marjorie Wutherspoon. The eyes, I think. Did you ever know her? Marjorie Wutherspoon, I mean, not the fish."

"No," said Perry, beckoning Jim, Doris and Brenda closer.

"A most entertaining woman, used to play one of the xylophones with Elspeth Kamitongo's Tropical Xylophonists. Equatorial melodies and the like. I've often wondered – oh, hello, you've brought associates."

Gerald Perry introduced everybody to Snorkel, who shook hands, wings and hoofs all round. "I've brought them to meet you on a matter of grave urgency."

"Grave urgency, eh?" said Snorkel, putting on his spectacles again and clasping his hands behind his back.

"Yes," said Jim. "We're hoping you might be able to help us with an underwater problem."

At the sound of the word "underwater", Teddy Snorkel's eyes lost their greyness and became a glittering light blue. "That's m'speciality, anything under the water," he grinned. He shuffled to his chair and sat. "Tell me all about it, sonny. What did you say his name was, Marjorie?" he asked Perry.

"Jim," said Perry, blushing.

"Memory's not the best any more, not since I've started forgetting things, but go on, tell me, tell me, John."

With mounting rapidity, Cairo Jim recounted the whole story again. Doris punctuated the telling every so often with a short squawk, usually whenever she thought Jim was wandering a bit off the track of the tale. All through it, Gerald Perry kept looking at the fish in the bowl and then at himself and then at the fish again, wondering what possible resemblance they had in common.

By the time Jim had almost finished talking, he was breathless. "I'm sorry if I seem to be blurting all of this out," he said, "it's just that I'm becoming concerned about the time factor. Bone's been down there an awful long time as it is, and I really think we should try and get to him as quickly as possible, just in case he *is* still in the land of the living."

"Neptune Bone, eh?" pondered Teddy Snorkel. "Can't say I remember him. Been a member of the Society for long?"

"About as long as I have," answered Jim. "He's exceedingly unfinancial."

"It's all very strange," said Teddy. "That beast you mentioned. Now I know that some men have different sorts of hobbies – model locomotives, and collecting grains of coloured sand, and spotting dirigibles – but *rubber sea serpents*? Sounds most depraved."

"It was depraved, all right," said Jim. "He was using it as a decoy, to keep people away while he was diving."

"What was he going after in the Red Sea? There's nothing there for an archaeologist, except fish and giant

70

slugs and predatory seahorses and other amphibious exotica."

"Sekheret," Jim said, and was about to explain that he was not offering anything to do with tobacco, when Snorkel interjected.

"*What did you say?*"

"I said Sekheret."

Teddy Snorkel's eyes brimmed with excitement. He turned quickly to Perry. "Oh, Marjorie, Marjorie, you have brought me my salvation!" He sprang up out of his chair and grasped Jim firmly by the shoulders. "My boy, you have breathed life into the hide of an old, forgetful man. Do you *know* of Pharaoh Sekheret?"

"We surely do," piped up Doris.

"Yes," replied Jim. "Doris, Brenda and myself study obscure Egyptian history by kerosene lamplight every evening in the Valley of the Kings. When we're not playing cards or reading, that is."

"Obscure's right," said Teddy Snorkel. "Most of them upstairs have long forgotten about Sekheret and his Dynasty. Even the events surrounding his felonious submergence. It's one of the few things I *do* remember. That blastratted Murray Savlon."

"Mmm," said Perry. "I'd have got to him with a wet—"

"I understand now why Bone was in the area. After old Sekheret's sarcophagus, eh? Why, it's one of the few royal caskets – known of, that is – that we don't have in the Cairo Museum. Oh, Jack, Jack, do you think he might have found it?"

 **71**

"I have no idea," Jim said. "But I think the only way to find out is for me to go down there after him. That's why we've come to see you."

"Ah," said Snorkel.

"Perry has told me of your innovative work in the field of aquatic archaeology, and I thought that maybe—"

Teddy Snorkel trembled like a wizened volcano. "At last!" he erupted. "At last, my work will be *of value*! All the theories and ideas and concepts on which I laboured and slaved will come in *useful*! Oh, Marjorie, thank you for bringing Cairo Jake and his friends here to me, although I think you should have a bit of a shave. That moustache doesn't suit you at all."

"I rather like it," said Perry, rubbing his moustache in an embarrassed sort of way.

"I was hoping, Mr Snorkel," said Jim, "you might have some equipment we could use – aqualungs and diving suits and waterproof thingummies."

"Oh, I most certainly do!" Teddy Snorkel rubbed his hands together enthusiastically. "Now, if I can only remember where I've put everything. Haven't gone much out of this room for a while. Hmm. Let me see – ah, yes. I recall I was working on a revolutionary new diving suit, fully adaptable for man, woman, bird or quadruped, shortly before I succumbed to the Final Frustration and came down here to Ponder. Where did I store everything? Let me think— Ah! I know! Follow me, if you will."

"Did you hear that?" Jim whispered to Doris and

Brenda. "Diving suits for the likes of both of you. How aquatically awesome!"

"I've never hard of anything more silly in all my feathered life," Doris grumbled. "Who ever heard of a *macaw* going deep-sea diving?"

"Don't you want to, Doris? Where's your sense of adventure?"

"If you want me to be a water bird, I'll wear a tuxedo and waddle, but I'm not—"

"Come on, you lot," called Gerald Perry, who had followed Teddy to the corner of the room.

"Coming, Marjorie," squawked Doris, and the trio quickly came to join them.

"Very droll," said Perry.

"Now, let's see," pondered Teddy. "Just through here, I think it was." He ran his hands across the wall, and at a certain spot parallel to the height of his chest he pressed both his palms firmly against the surface. He did this no less than six times.

"What's he doing?" whispered Doris. "Press-ups?"

With a hushed whoosh, a section of the wall slid away to create a hole the size and shape of a narrow doorway. Beyond this lay an oblong-shaped room, lit up by a skylight of strengthened glass laid into the sidewalk above.

All around the room lay travelling trunks and tea chests and hat boxes and old suitcases of varying sizes with dusty baggage stickers all over them.

"Come on in, my friends," Teddy Snorkel said.

"What's all this clutter?" asked Perry.

"My life, I suppose," sighed Snorkel. "Everything I've ever done, or dreamed about, or invented. Plus a few too many things I never got the *chance* to do or dream or invent." He scratched his tangled curls and squinted through his spectacles. "Now, where *was* it? Hmmm."

As everyone watched, he went from travelling trunk to tea chest to suitcase, opening each one in turn and inspecting the contents. Sometimes he would pull a few objects out and look at them confusedly or fondly before putting them back and closing the lid; sometimes he would close a lid as soon as he had opened it, most usually with the hat boxes.

After a few minutes, he straightened his back and gave a small squeak. "Eureka! Found it, Marjorie, old girl."

He turned around, smiling proudly, holding his hands at shoulder height. Out of his fists draped a full-body-length swimsuit of the sleekest, silveriest material Jim, Doris or Brenda had ever seen. It was as silver as a needle and as slender as a straw.

"This was the prototype for what should've been the most revolutionary, water-breaking, elbow-boggling deep-sea swimsuit in the history of aquatica," Teddy Snorkel announced. "Why, if m'funding had come through, we would have had people exploring the ocean's bottom as effortlessly as they explore their own kitchen pantries. Here, Cairo Jock, let me hold it up against you. See how it fits."

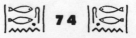

He held it against Jim's shoulders and Jim took it from his grip.

"Perfect fit, length-wise," said Gerald Perry. "It's so light," Jim said, rubbing his thumbs and forefingers over the suit. "Hardly any weight in it at all."

Teddy smiled. "Invented that material m'self, you know. "Gaudy Gossamer", I called it. If you think it's light *now*, just wait until you get it under the sea. Loses fifty per cent of its present weight when it comes into contact with H_2O." He chuckled proudly.

"Well, swoggle me swiftly with a sea sponge," gasped Jim.

Doris flapped over to Jim's waist and peered at a narrow strip of small, liquid-crystal screens that ran around the outfit like a belt on a pair of trousers. "Rarrk! What's this?"

"Oh," said Teddy. "Just a second." He slid a minuscule switch on the suit's shoulder, near Jim's thumb (Jim took special notice of this), and the liquid-crystal screens in the belt all lit up brilliantly.

Numbers and diagrams and symbols flashed across the displays, and there came soft but urgent beeps and noises that sounded like electronic caterpillars scuttling across pianos.

After half a minute the noises stopped abruptly, and the small screens settled down until there was a single image steadily displayed upon each one.

"For the love of Hatshepsut," muttered Gerald Perry Esquire.

"That one there," said Teddy, pointing to one of the screens, "tells you how deep you've gone, in fathoms, I think it is. That screen tells you how many hours, minutes and seconds you've been submerged, and will beep twice every fifteen minutes. That screen gives you the temperature of the water; that screen warns you of any invading predators – it picks up on their hostile vibrations and makes a high-pitched squeak; that screen will display how much oxygen you have left in your supply; and that screen tells you what time it is in Helsinki. I used to wonder about that all the time when *I* was diving, for some reason."

"Speaking of oxygen, where are the tanks?"

"Tanks?" said Teddy, as though Jim had just uttered a rude word. "Tanks? M'boy, there're no tanks connected to this aquatic apparel. No, indeed. All your oxygen is contained in the cranium cover. Now, there's one here somewhere, if I'm not mistaken." He turned and bent over one of the trunks, and Doris watched as his bottom wriggled about like it was involved in some sort of slow, rhythmical samba dance. "Ah! Gotcha! Here, Cairo Tim, slip this onto your bonce."

Now everybody was truly amazed, for they had all been expecting Snorkel to extricate an enormous, cumbersome helmet the likes of which would have been able to contain one or possibly two long oxygen cylinders. Instead, he gave Jim a small skullcap of burnished silver, with underwater goggles built in. Jim draped the suit along one of the travelling trunks and eased the cap onto

his head. It fitted as though it was a second scalp.

"But what about the oxygen supply?" asked Doris, stretching her neck and sounding troubled. "Run your fingers around inside the cap, just behind where your ears are," Teddy instructed.

Jim did so. "Goodness, there are two little bumps," he said.

"Inside those little bumps sit two capsules of concentrated oxygen." Teddy held out his hand and showed what looked like a small aspirin tablet. "It took me seven years to develop this, but finally, when I worked out the way to capture oxygen and shrink it so that it could fit into these small tablets, I succeeded. In each tablet there is enough oxygen to last for four hours. With two in your cap you can remain underwater for eight hours. Then, when one tablet runs out, you just pop another one in."

"But, how does the oxygen alter from tablet to gas?"

"Easy," smiled Teddy. "You see, the outer coating of the tablet is a mixture of gelatine and salt. Once it comes into contact with water, it slowly begins to dissolve. The oxygen inside the tablet then escapes into the tight-fitting headpiece, where it finds its only means of escape is through this tube at the front. Just there, next to where your mouth is, you see? That tube has a special regulatory device concealed within it which is only operable by the diver. It's quite simple, really: whenever you have a bit of a suck on the tube, you get as much oxygen as you want."

"Absolutely brilliant." Gerald Perry clapped his hands.

"Thank you, Marjorie. Your xylophony served as my inspiration."

"Mr Snorkel," said Jim, "May we use your prototypes to find Bone?"

"Use them to find Sekheret," answered Teddy. "If you find Bone, all very well, but the Pharaoh's casket is the real treasure."

"You mentioned you had suits for birds and quadrupeds," Perry said.

"Ooh, upon my word." He rummaged about for a bit and pulled out a small suit, just as silver as the first, but with extra long flappy bits at the side, and a sharp long extension built into the cap. "Here's the ornithological model," he announced. "I was working on a theory at the time about the compatibility that should exist between birds and fish. I'm not talking penguins or cormorants and the like; I mean the other, unaquatic birds in the realm. There are many things both species could learn from each other, if only they could inhabit the same environment. I thought it would've been easier to get our feathered friends down there rather than the scaled ones up here."

Doris took one look at the suit and felt her stomach go sluggish. "Er – very nice, I'm sure," she squawked. "Couldn't I just watch from above?"

"And here's the camel variety. What's old Bertha there? One hump or two?"

"Bactrian," said Jim, to which Brenda gave two snorts.

"Good-oh. Here it is. I developed this because camels shouldn't be deprived. Ugh." With a grunt he pulled out a much larger quantity of the silver material, all folded in neat layers, and a cap which had ample ear room. "Hope the hump cavities don't pinch."

Jim shook out the suit and laid it over Brenda's humps. The Wonder Camel felt a tingle zither up and down her mane.

"And here." Teddy gave Jim a small bottle. "There's a hundred oxygen tablets in there. Should be plenty."

"Thank you very much indeed." Jim reached out and shook Teddy Snorkel's hand. "We'll take the best care of everything."

"You've already taken the best care of an old archaeologist's heart," the old man smiled.

"Now," said Perry, "we'd best be off. We've used up a lot of time already, and there's no telling how much – or how little – of that precious commodity Neptune Bone has left."

"One question," interrupted Doris. She had been poking about Jim's suit, and Brenda's, and her own, and had discovered on all three of them a small piece of waterproof string with a brass ring dangling at the end of it. These were hanging from the back of the liquid-crystal-display-screen belts. "What're these strings for?"

"Those?" said Snorkel, picking up the ring of one and looking at it in a puzzled manner. "Hmm. Maybe

they're – no, couldn't be that. Perhaps they're – no, I'd never have put one of those in there. Let me think. Goodness me, would you believe it, I think I've forgotten."

"Yes," said Gerald Perry Esquire, ushering his friends out and trying to walk as unlike Marjorie Wutherspoon as he could. "I'd believe it *readily*."

"Best not touch them if you don't know what they do," shouted Teddy Snorkel as they were leaving. "First rule of ballet, that!"

CHAPTER 7

A BRUSH WITH THE SQUAD

ON THE FRONT STEPS of the Old Relics Society, Jim, Doris and Brenda bade their farewells to Gerald Perry Esquire (who, through a combination of flabellums notions and continual mention of Marjorie Wutherspoon, was now inflicted with severe twitches in the muscles underneath his eyebrows). As Perry shuffled back into the vestibule, Jim began to pack the diving suits carefully into Brenda's saddlebags.

"Goodness me," he said to Doris, who was perching on Brenda's nether hump. "Fancy old Teddy shutting himself away like that, when he clearly has so much to offer to the world. I wonder what drove him to become a recluse."

"'To thine own self be true'," quoted the macaw, "'and it must follow, as the night the day, thou canst not then be false to any man'."

Jim looked at her and smiled.

"*Hamlet*," she informed him. "Polonius's advice to his son, Laertes."

"What a learned bird you are," he said, fastening down the last strap on Brenda's saddle. He put on his pith helmet and looked at the Cutterscrog Old Timers Archaeological Timepiece on his wrist. "Right," he

announced. "Let's get a shake on. We haven't got time to waste, if we're to be successful in our quest."

Brenda gave an urgent snort, high and panicky, and Jim hoisted himself up onto her back. "It's all right, my lovely," he said, patting her neck, "we're on our way now."

Again she snorted urgently, the panic bristling through her mane. Jim tried to rein her around so she could descend the steps, but to no avail; the Wonder Camel would not move.

"Brenda, what is it?"

"Come on, Brenda," Doris screeched. "We're wasting time."

"Quaaaooooo!"

"Whatever is the matter?" Jim looked around at Doris. "I think she's upset at something, my dear."

Doris fluttered her wing delicately over Brenda's haunches. "What's up, you hesitant thing?"

Brenda rolled her head towards one of the creamy granite pillars, and Jim and Doris followed her direction. "It's only a pillar, Brenda," said Jim. "You've seen hundreds of the things, here in Cairo and in the Valleys of the Kings and Queens and Hairdressers. There's nothing to be alarmed about."

"Rark! Jim, look!"

From behind the pillar, a small cloud of smoke appeared. It wafted languidly away, off into the air, until the afternoon sunlight broke it up into a thousand wisps, each of them as thin as a human hair.

For a few seconds everything was still. Then Jim

cleared his throat. "Excuse me," he called to the pillar. "Whoever's loitering behind that pillar, would you please come out and show yourself. You're scaring my friend here."

Another small cloud of smoke wafted out from behind the pillar, and this time, before it dispersed, a tall, thin man appeared wearing a white linen suit, crumpled in just the right places, and a mulberry-coloured fez with a black tassel (uncrumpled). He removed his meerschaum pipe from his grim lips and nodded his head to the trio.

"Good afternoon," came his formal tone.

"Good afternoon," said Jim, and Doris squawked something in Spanish. Brenda quickly calmed down.

"Allow me to introduce myself to you all," the man said. "You are probably thinking that I am Basil Rathbone, the film actor. Many people notice the resemblance, usually in the latter throes of the day, and in the evenings whenever I am standing in a light that is mellow. There is a similarity, I admit it, although I am altogether much more swarthy. But no, I am not Basil Rathbone. If you thought I was, I am sorry to disappoint you."

"Well, no," Jim said, looking again at his Cutterscrog.

"I am" – and he produced from his breast pocket a brown leather wallet which fell open to reveal a photograph of himself standing in a light that was indeed very mellow – "Inspector Mustafa Kuppa of the Antiquities Squad, Maxwell House Branch. You

may have heard of me, Cairo Jim. I have certainly heard of *you*, and may I say what an earnest pleasure it is to meet you after so long. You are a credit to your profession."

"Thank you, Inspector Kuppa. It's nice to meet you, also, but if you don't mind, we must trot away. We have some urgent business to attend to in the south-east."

"One momentum, if you please." Kuppa closed his wallet, put it back into his pocket, and came to Brenda's side. "This encounter is not merely a coincidence. My office knew you were here, and I have come along to speak with you about a most serious matter. Because I am not a member of the Old Relics Society I was not permitted to enter these hallowed halls, and so I have spent a considerable part of my most valuable afternoon waiting for you here on these introductory steps. The glare from all this creaminess" – he gestured to the pillars – "has caused me the most rotten headache."

"What can we do for you, Inspector?"

"I have reason to believe that you, Cairo Jim, may know of the whereabouts of that dubious archaeologist, Captain Neptune F. Bone. Is this true?"

"I don't know where he is," Jim answered in all truth.

"Are you quite sure?" The earlier formal cordiality in Kuppa's voice was now replaced with a knifelike seriousness. "As you are no doubt aware from reading the newspapers, Captain Bone is wanted by the Antiquities Squad. He has been up to some very unpleasant, not to mention wonky, activities."

"I am quite sure I don't know exactly where he is. Why, as far as I'm aware, he may not still even be in Egypt."

"Hmm." Kuppa took a long suck on his pipe and arched his left eyebrow (an action he believed made him look *very* much like Basil Rathbone). "Answer me this, Cairo Jim: what is your urgent business in the south-east? What does it involve?"

Jim could feel Doris fidgeting behind him on Brenda's saddle. "Jim," she prowked, "the day is slipping away from us. Can't we just ride off?"

"Wait a moment, my dear."

"I beg your pardon, Cairo Jim?"

"Not you, Inspector Kuppa."

"Oh." He sounded disappointed. "You haven't answered my question: what is so important for you in the south-east?"

"Sekheret."

"No, thank you all the same, I only smoke this pipe. It is the same model that Sherlock—"

"*Pharaoh* Sekheret." Jim was by now exasperated. "Look, Inspector Kuppa, I'm very sorry we can't help you with some concrete information about Neptune Bone, but we really must be going." He swung Brenda's neck towards Talaat Harb Street.

"I understand, Cairo Jim. Wait, there is one more thing I must ask you!"

"What, Inspector?" Brenda was stepping carefully down the stairs.

"Where can I contact your good self if anything turns up regarding Bone? You may want to be notified."

"We'll be somewhere around Hurghada," shouted Jim, as Brenda entered the traffic. "Red Sea district!"

"I will remember that, Cairo Jim," Inspector Mustafa Kuppa muttered to himself as he impatiently massaged his temples.

"But Jim," squawked Doris, as Brenda trotted heedfully through the vehicles surrounding them, "why didn't you just tell Kuppa where Bone *might* be? It would've saved us an awful lot of bother, not to mention wet feathers." Her beak winced.

"You won't get wet feathers with these suits," smiled Jim. "I had good reason not to divulge too much to Kuppa. You see, I hope we *will* find Bone, and if we do, we'll hand him over to the Antiquities Squad as soon as they come to get him. But there's also a chance we might find the royal sarcophagus. If that happens, we want it to go straight to the Old Relics Society, rather than the Antiquities Squad first."

"But why?" Doris's plumage bristled testily. "Both places'll do the same thing: they'll clean it and restore it if it needs to be restored, and catalogue it, and then they'll place it in the Cairo Museum for everyone to be able to view. What difference will it make *who* gets it first? Rarrk."

"A lot. You see, my dear, the Society comprises members who have a great passion for the past. Most of

us are archaeologists – active and retired – and we all have a great concern that artefacts should be made available for all to see. Now, I'm sure there are some people in the Antiquities Squad who feel the same way, but unfortunately the Antiquities Squad is a bureaucracy. Things just don't happen quickly in a place like that."

"What's a bureaucracy?" spluttered the macaw.

"A place where people fill in forms, and write letters and memoranda, and where paper mounts up until it rubs against the ceiling. Where the wheels of progress turn very slowly, so slowly they almost go backwards. If the sarcophagus ended up there first, there's no telling how long it would take before all the work was done and the sarcophagus could go on display in the Museum."

"Coo," cooed Doris, thinking once again how strange human beings were.

The turnoff to the Pyramids Road was looming before them, and Jim gave Brenda a gentle prod with his heel. "Gee up, my lovely," he shouted, and the mighty Wonder Camel took off as though she had turbo blasters in her rear hoofs.

ᘃᗡᗩᘐᑌ 8 ᘃᗡᗩᘐᑌ
TAKING THE PLUNGE

BACK BY THE SHORE of the Red Sea, Doris was not at all keen on the idea of what was about to happen. She waddled about on the sand, a distasteful scowl upon her beak. Her diving suit was lying in a heap on the ground, and occasionally she gave it a half-hearted little kick with her claw, while Jim and Brenda were struggling into their outfits.

"Don't see why I need to go down as well," the macaw grumbled. "The both of you should be enough. You'll have two sets of eyes, after all. *And* Brenda's Wondrous Instincts. I don't see why *I'm* required."

Jim, who was half-in and half-out of his apparel, frowned at her. "My dear, I certainly don't want to make you go down if you don't want to."

"Rerk! Doesn't seem right, that's all. It goes against nature. Thou birds in the sky, thou fish in the sea, thou fox in his lair, 'tis how things should be."

"Mr Shakespeare?"

"No, Ms Doris. The whole concept's as silly as a hatful of worms. It makes my feathers hackle."

"Doris, you shouldn't worry. I have no doubt that Teddy's suits will stand the test of the waters. You'll probably find that once you're down there, it'll be just

 **88**

like flying, only with water around you instead of air."

"Hmmph." She kicked at her diving suit again.

Jim hitched his silvery suit up, and wriggled his left shoulder into it. "Look," he said to Doris, "if you'd really rather, you can stay here and wait for us. I understand. But" – and he looked at her with pleading eyebrows – "it won't be the same down there without you. Brenda and I'll be okay, I'm sure, but without you – well, we're a team, aren't we? You, Brenda and me. All the digs we've been through, all those places we've visited. Peru, Greece, Emnobellia, the Ivory Coast, the Valley of the Kings. Why, the three of us have always been together. Isn't that right, Brenda?"

Brenda, who had managed to get her head stuck in one of her suit's hump cavities, gave an agreeing (although harassed) snort.

"My dear, if you must know, I really don't want to go down there without you. It just wouldn't be – right. You're indispensable to me, Doris. There, I've said it!"

Doris stopped waddling and kicking and arched the feathers above her right eye. "Do you mean that?" she blinked.

"You can concrete my legs together and call me an obelisk if I don't," answered Jim.

"Reerarrk!" She flapped her huge wings together in a clapping motion, and their gold and blue hues blazed in the sunlight. "Why didn't you say so before? Come on, what are we waiting for? The sooner we find Bone and the sarcophagus, the sooner we'll be back on terra firma!"

And with a gleam in her eye (and being careful that her beak didn't thwang up into her face), she busied herself with her suit.

Jim gave Brenda a wink.

Soon Jim and Doris were fully enclosed in their silvery cocoons. Brenda was still having some difficulty getting into hers, so the two went to give her a hand and wing. It took a bit of doing, on account of the different design of Brenda's suit, but soon her humps were snug, and her ears were covered in their earflaps, and her tail had slid into the thin tail-tube at the rear.

Doris fluttered underneath the Wonder Camel's belly to check that all the zippers were fastened. "Hmm," she said, noticing the waterproof string with the brass ring dangling at the end of it. "We still don't know what these are for, do we?"

"No," frowned Jim, lifting the one attached to his suit. "Remember what Teddy said: don't touch it if you don't know what it does. Right, my friends. Time for oxygen."

He reached down to Brenda's saddlebag lying on the sand and took out the bottle of oxygen tablets. Unscrewing the cap, he tipped twenty tablets into the palm of his silver-gloved hand. He replaced the cap, put fourteen of the tablets into a pocket he had found behind the elbow of his suit, and put the bottle back into the saddlebag.

With tension pulsing through his jaw he pulled the elasticised cranium cover away from his right cheek and

snaked his fingers towards his ear. Pressed between his fingertips and the side of his head was a single tablet of oxygen. With a bit of careful fiddling – it was the tightest squeeze in here, on account of the close-fitting cranium cover – he found the small area at the back of his ears, the area where the tablet was meant to reside, and popped it in place. He slowly removed his fingers and repeated the process on the other side of his head.

When he had done this he did the same for Doris. Although the bird didn't have any ears like a human's, Teddy Snorkel had still made provision for the tablets by sewing two small half-pockets in the inside of her cranium cover, just behind where her hearing-holes were.

"Rerark! It's snug, isn't it?" Doris flexed her wings and gave her tail plumage (encased in its sleek silver membrane) an uncertain shake. "Feels like I'm covered in that plastic filmy stuff Mrs Amun-Ra puts over her pinkies when we take them home with us."

"I'm sure," Jim said as he inserted Brenda's oxygen tablets behind her earflaps, "that you won't even notice it when you're down below. Remember, according to Teddy these suits lose half their weight when they come into contact with water." He stepped back from Brenda and rubbed his silver-gloved hands together. With no warning, a rippling tingle of electricity oscillated up and down his spine, and he recognised it to be the old familiar excitement that always greeted him at the very beginning of a major expedition.

"Okey-dokey, my friends," he smiled – it was a handsome, confident smile, full of promise and mystery – "let's venture forth, before that appalling raven comes to annoy us."

"Too right," blinked Doris, pulling her beakpiece into position, and her goggles down across her eyes.

"Quaaoo," snorted Brenda, wrapping her huge lips around her snout-piece.

Jim put his desert sun-spectacles inside his pith helmet, which he then put on his head, on top of his cranium cover, and strapped it firmly down underneath his chin. He pulled his goggles over his eyes and took his mouth-piece in his fingers.

"Activate your suits," he instructed, before popping the mouth-piece where it fitted best.

The three of them slid the minuscule switches on their shoulder, wing, and brisket, and their liquid-crystal-screen belts all came to life with those same electronic-caterpillars-scuttling-across-pianos noises. The noises quickly died away, and the screens settled down to their constant, steady displays.

"Look," shrieked Doris (a bit garbled because of her beak-piece). "It's three o'clock in Helsinki!"

Jim strode towards the lapping waterline, his brass ring dangling at the end of the waterproof string. "Come on then," he called over his shoulder. "Every minute counts now."

Doris fluttered and Brenda lumbered after him, and soon they were disappearing beneath the still surface of

 92

the Red Sea, unaware of the mocking, throbbing eyeballs of the flea-infested raven who had been watching them for the past twenty minutes.

The water was cool, but not cold, and remarkably clear. As Jim trod carefully on the ever-descending ocean floor, he thought how easy it was to see ahead of him. There were no weeds or shell fragments or oily patches to obliterate their vision. The water was so clean it was almost transparent, and Jim had to remind himself after some minutes that he was actually beneath the surface of the sea, and not out in the fresh invisible air of their familiar earthly environment.

Deeper and deeper and deeper they went, step by step, minute by minute. The water became nothing more than their usual surroundings; it did not worry them or make them nervous.

For Doris, this new place was an unexpected pleasure, and she took to it like another member of her species takes to water. With even less effort than she used above ground, she was able to beat her wings and swim along. The only difference between her normal flying and this new swimming caper was the small bubbles that whooshed away from her wingtips.

And there was something else that pleased her: she was able to perform the most beautiful curved swoops, as graceful as water in a fountain, never having to worry about the wind that often prevented this sort of clever flying if she were above the ground. Here there was no

wind, just the occasional gentle current that was not strong enough to throw her off her course.

The beautiful silver bird began to fly-swim backwards and forwards, swooping and diving around Jim and Brenda, and obliviously imagining that she was one of those synchronised human swimmers, with glistening goggles and pearly-teeth smiles, whom she had once seen at a special aquatics display Jim had taken her to in Cairo.

Brenda, too, was enjoying the strange new sensations of total submergence. She found that her movements were only slowed a little, and she relished the feeling of the cool water against the outside of her suit, while inside she was warm and dry as a silkworm. She felt secure and wildly adventurous – even more so than when she read her Melodious Tex novels – and her humps tingled agreeably.

Shortly after their heads had been covered by the water, they had all been aware of a small fizzing taking place behind their ears and hearing-holes. Jim smiled and gestured at where his oxygen tablets were concealed. Doris nodded, and Brenda tried to snort, an action she was not going to repeat for the duration of their underwater activities as it led to a most unpleasant burst of bubbles up her snout.

After almost fifteen minutes of moving ahead on the descending floor, Jim stopped abruptly. He gestured to Doris and Brenda to do likewise, and to come and join him. They both did so.

"Look down there," Jim motioned with his eyes.

They followed his gaze and both of them gulped. Two steps away from the tips of Jim's silver boots, the ocean floor disappeared. It didn't just dwindle off, or become a rubbley, gravelly slope – it simply was *not there*. The floor beneath them stopped as suddenly as a gun shot rings out on a silent afternoon, and there was nothing but a magnificently deep chasm, wherein the water was dark and murky.

Jim peered into the abyss and wondered how they would see in all that darkness. As he took a step closer to the edge, one of the liquid-crystal-display screens in his belt zapped on with a beam of halogen light, which shone straight ahead in a crisp, brilliant shaft. It lit up the dimness so it was as clear as the water to which they were so far accustomed.

Doris waddled forward, and an identical beam shot out from her belt. She turned to Brenda and, when her back was to the darkness, her halogen light blinked off. She turned back to face the darkness and the light snapped on again. She did this three or four times, the light blinking on and off every time, pretending she was a lighthouse and warning ships off the rocks, but looking more like some sort of indecisive firefly doing the Watusi.

Brenda thought a snort, and she stepped forward. Instantly her belt zapped on its light.

Jim smiled as he thought what a true genius that man Snorkel was.

Down below, with all three lights exploring the chasm, the water appeared to be clear, but the deeper the chasm became, the more it filled with shadows. The shadowy shapes near the bottom seemed to be moving, slowly back and forth and up and down, with no sound whatsoever.

Cairo Jim looked at his companions and raised his eyebrows. Both Doris and Brenda nodded.

The three of them joined hand, wings and hoof (Doris was in the centre) and, gently stepping off the edge of the ocean floor, they began sinking silently to the shadowy depths.

UNDERNEATH THE PERCHES

DOWN THEY FLOATED, steadily and heavily, as the temperature of the water became cooler and cooler. After several minutes they began to descend upon what looked like hundreds of tall, thin, haphazard towers rising up from the floor of the chasm. These resembled high piles of solidified feathery rocks, or steeples of cake-icing which had formed drip by drip. Doris let go of Jim's hand and Brenda's hoof and swooped down to inspect them. After several looks she came back to Jim and shrugged her wings.

Jim took his finger and traced out an imaginary word upon his silver sleeve. First a C, followed by ORAL.

Doris, who had never seen a coral reef before, looked suitably impressed.

They continued to float downwards, the towers of coral looming above them. Just as they were about to land on the chasm floor – or what appeared to be the chasm floor, it was very hard to tell where things started and finished down here – a school of small, triangular-shaped fish whizzed past so quickly that the current made by their path lifted Brenda's tail-tube. The fish were striped in orange, yellow, and electric green, and as Jim's belt-light swung around to illuminate them, their tiny eyeballs

popped in alarm. In less than an instant the whole school changed its course and darted bubblingly away.

These were the first of many fish they were to see, and by no means the smallest. There were fish the size of darning needles, all neon-bright yellow, with minuscule heads and mouths; fish as fat as legs of ham, coloured like a spotted eiderdown Jim had used as a boy; long, slender, glossy fish, purple with pinkish gills; fish with huge lips, and fins like long ribbons of silk wafting in the current.

It occurred to Jim that all of these fish's colours were so widespread it was as though some god had grabbed hold of a spare rainbow and dunked it into the sea, causing the pigments to run in the water and stain the creatures below. Jim decided that this notion was rather poetic, and that when they were above ground again he would concoct a verse or two about it.

His thoughts of being above ground made him remember his purpose for coming down here, and he moved his mind away from the beautiful dazzlingness of the fish and onto the more real (and less attractive) reality of Neptune Bone. With this odious subject uppermost in his mind, he began to inspect the fine white sand littering the floor.

While he was engaged in this, Brenda was plodding about by herself near a particularly impressive coral edifice which looked a bit like an oversized lavatory brush. She was moving around, minding her own business, when suddenly she stepped on something soft

and spongy and slimy. She reared back, bubbles flying up from beneath her belly, as the thing below cavorted and sludged around. It opened its drooling mouth, and a wrinkle of sponginess parted to reveal a beady slimy eye. The two-and-a-half-metre giant sea slug saw Brenda and, unable to comprehend her size and shape, it slabbered sulkily away into the gloom.

(There was another dark and slabbery something lying not far away, its extensive and ancient girth coiled around the wavering towers of coral. It opened one eye at all this bubbly fuss, saw what was going on, and slowly closed it again, hoping that the lumpy, silvery fish with legs would not come to bother it.)

Doris, meanwhile, had come across a shoal of parrot fish and was trying to start up some sort of conversation with them. As she couldn't screech or squawk down here, she was trying to communicate through miming and charades. It didn't appear to be going very well, as the bewildered parrot fish only stared at her with open beaks and wide eyes, trying to figure out why this silver-beaked being was gesticulating so oddly and pretending she was trapped behind some sort of wall when there clearly wasn't one there in the first place.

Jim was poking about near some coral and enormous clam shells, when his eye fixed on something that didn't seem to belong. He reached down and picked it up. He looked at it carefully, turning it over this way and that in his glove. He squeezed it gently. Then he motioned to Doris and Brenda.

They came immediately (Doris being glad of the excuse to leave the uncommunicative parrot fish), and Jim held the object out before them. The macaw and Wonder Camel regarded it curiously.

It was a piece of black hose, about three centimetres long. One end of it was ragged, as though it had been severed quickly, or chewed through.

Jim gestured to his mouth, and then to the piece of hose. Then he held both arms out from his body so that he appeared basketball-shaped, and then he made an imaginary cylinder shape with his hands on top of his pith helmet.

Doris and Brenda knew who he meant.

They began to scour the sandy floor for further signs of Bone. After only two minutes, Brenda stamped her hoof, giving rise to a shaft of bubbles. Jim and Doris joined her to see what had caused her excitement.

There by her hoof were two footprints: large, heavy, squarish footprints, the sort made by old-fashioned diving boots. Next to these, the sand had been swirled all around, as though a maelstrom had taken place. Next to this, a long drag mark had been made. It disappeared into the coral, and on either side of it there were two sets of fin-shaped prints.

"You clever beast," thought Jim as he smiled at her. Then he frowned. They were obviously standing at the scene of some sort of struggle, where the victim had been overpowered and bundled off. Jim waved his arms about, pretended to punch himself, and pointed at the

marks on the ground. He then pointed off into the coral, in the direction of the dragging trail.

Doris and Brenda nodded, and Doris alone took a big gulp and thought it was a good thing that Jim could not fully see her face and the worried expression on it.

Jim led the way. For half an hour they waded and swam further and further into the coral, following the dragging trail and the finprints along paths that had been worn by unknown giant molluscs and other creatures, until they found themselves in what Jim imagined was the centre of the coral forest. Here the dragging trail ended.

The archaeologist-poet blinked and frowned. The finprints had disappeared! They had not wandered off, but had ceased completely, for what appeared to be no reason at all. Nor did the drag mark go any further, but remained there, a messy testament to an abrupt mystery.

Cairo Jim turned to the right and to the left, and his halogen light spread in both directions. Nothing. It was as though whoever was responsible for this trail had evaporated from the very face of the ocean.

A flurry of bubbles caught Jim's and Doris's attention. They quickly swam to the source: on a smooth rock, surrounded by reeds, stood Brenda, her head bent low.

Doris swivelled her hips to where Brenda was looking. There, illuminated by the light from her belt, stretched a channel – a rough, pebbled channel, wider than a dozen twenty-lane highways – that rose up steeply into the darkness of the waters above. Near to where this channel joined Brenda's rock, they were able to discern, amongst

the scattered pebbles, the same drag marks and finprints they had been pursuing.

Jim smiled and nodded, and, jumping from Brenda's rock, began to lead the way up the rising pebbled channel.

It was a steep climb, and occasionally Brenda had trouble with the skiddy pebbles, but with the help of her two friends she was able to make good progress. As they rose higher and higher, Jim kept an eye on the finprints, which were easier to see than the drag mark was, amongst the mess of stones.

Soon, ahead of and above them, they could see a horizontal line. It seemed to be hanging in the water, and dipping back and forth slightly, in the same way a seesaw rises and falls. The line confounded Jim; he could not work out what it was, or why it was hanging there before them. They kept moving towards it, getting closer and closer with every step, until, with a sudden shock, he discovered *exactly* what it was.

With a single step (and a beat of Doris's wings), all three of them broke the lapping line, emerging swiftly up into the space above and beyond it. As they did so, the line moved down their heads, necks and torsos, until it was at their feet, claws and hoofs. Then, with another step, it was behind them.

They were no longer beneath water.

Jim removed his oxygen-sucking tube and lifted his goggles. "Well, blow me down with a papyrus reed," he said. "We're dry again!"

"Rark," screeched Doris, and the screech echoed off and away into the colossal chamber in which they now stood. "Where are we?"

"Your guess is as good as mine, my dear." He inspected their surroundings. "We're not above ground, yet at the same time we're not below the sea. Hmm."

"Quaaooo," snorted Brenda, happy to be able to make some sort of noise after having had a bit of rubber pipe stuck in her gob for so long.

"We've climbed quite a distance," said Jim, looking down through the waterline – the line they had broken through – at the now blurry channel they had ascended.

Doris peered up at the towering walls surrounding them, which looked as though they formed a natural dome at the top. "Limestone, if I'm not mistaken," she squawked.

"So it is," agreed Jim.

"Quaaoo!"

"What, my lovely? Doris, look, Brenda's found the rest of the channel." He stepped away in that direction. "Come on, gang, it looks like dry sailing from here on in."

He started scrambling eagerly up the incline, rising higher and higher towards the domed ceiling of the chamber. Doris jumped on Brenda's fore hump, and they climbed quickly after him.

The channel climbed at a constant steepness, until it stopped at a point very close to the ceiling of the chamber. When Jim was at the very top, at the last point where he could stand fully before hitting his pith helmet

against the ceiling, he stopped and looked ahead. And his jaw dropped open, far wider than it had ever been in his life.

In front of him, spread out as far as his naked eye could see, was a broader, higher dome, made of the same brilliant limestone as the first. It was wider than the bases of a dozen pyramids.

"I'll be swoggled," he muttered.

The dome was glinting with the reflections of hundreds of tiny lights shining up from below. Jim looked down, and his heart started beating a Ha-Cha-Cha rhythm that would have made an orchestra leader proud. His legs became unsteady, his hands became so moist they started to fill his gloves with liquid, and his eyebrows prickled like a porcupine's.

There before him, stretched out to the very ends of the limestone dome, at the end of the channel path which sloped down and away, lay an ancient city!

Jim was too overcome, as he stared at the hundreds of ornate, flat-roofed buildings and leaning towers and sunken gardens and shining roadways and all the great architecture that lay before him, to speak a single syllable. The beauty of it all; the dreams and visions and breathtaking confidence that had gone into the creation of this civilisation was astounding, and he knew immediately where he was.

Doris and Brenda had by now caught up, and they too were overwhelmed. After a few moments, Doris turned to her friend. "'There is a world elsewhere'," she

cooed, quoting from *Coriolanus*. "Where are we, Jim?" she asked quietly.

"Atlantis," whispered Cairo Jim.

"Is this *Atlantis*?" squawked Doris. "That's what Bone was trying to write!"

Brenda's eyes were moist, and it wasn't from the ocean they had left behind.

Jim's voice was so light it barely left his throat. "It was always supposed that everything that was Atlantis was plunged below the ocean because of an earthquake. The force must've been so very great, so fast and furious, that the whole city was sucked up the channel and into this place here." His eyes travelled across all that was below. "I wouldn't be surprised if we've just come up the entrance to some hollow, undersea mountain."

"Rark?"

"By some colossal freak of nature, the channel must have been made at such a gradient that water can't rise up it past a certain point. I remember reading about this sort of thing when I was at Archaeology School. This kind of underwater phenomenon can only happen when the surrounding area is put under an almost unbearable amount of natural stress – such as that caused by a huge disruption – an earthquake or landslide, for example." He thought for a few moments. "Of course! It was always thought that an *undersea* quake was the cause for the sinking of Atlantis!"

He looked back down upon the city as it lay in a dim but steady amber glow, the illumination coming from

the lamps burning on window ledges and pedestals in the streets. "I never thought—" he muttered. "I never ever thought or dreamed—"

Right at that moment, their belts started squeaking, loudly and urgently. The lights in them flashed on and off like hiccuping lightning.

"*Raarrk*!" screamed Doris, as two rough seaweed-nets thumped down over her and Brenda. "Help, Jim!"

"*Quaaaooo*!" bellowed the Wonder Camel.

"What the—?" cried Jim, spinning around, just in time to see another wall of netting being flung straight at him.

Part Two:

ANTEDILUVIAN REALM

SOUR-FACED AND SEARCHING

THE MAN with the self-proclaimed resemblance to Basil Rathbone the film actor threw open the passenger door of his Alvis squad car and stepped elegantly out onto the hot, white sand.

He stood silently, his gaze scanning the great expanse of Red Sea before him, the tassel of his fez blowing limply in the wind. There was no noise coming from the water, and no activity visible upon it.

Inspector Mustafa Kuppa took out his meerschaum pipe and put it to his mouth. He lit a match and, pausing only to tamp down the tobacco with his thumb, put the flame into the bowl. This, he thought sulkily, would be his only companion while he searched – and waited – for his prey. That pith-helmeted archaeologist with the penchant for poetry knew more than he was letting on, thought Kuppa, throwing the dead match disdainfully into the breeze.

Then, partly because of the emptiness surrounding him and partly because he liked the sound of his own voice, he spoke loudly to himself:

"Neptune Bone is lurking somewhere in this vicinity, or I'm not a master Antiquities Detective. It is just a matter of time, just a matter of—"

An object lying forlorn and isolated in the cleft between two sand hills halted his speech. He reached into his automobile and took out his Departmental Binoculars (for which he had had to complete nine separate forms, documents and receipts before being allowed to take them from Maxwell House headquarters). Quickly he raised them to his Hollywood-style sun-spectacles and focussed them onto the object.

"Hmm," he declared, as if he were doing a voice audition for a movie. "If that's not the macramé saddle and bags worn by that camel of Cairo Jim's, then I'm Dorothy Carless."*

He lowered the binoculars and hung them around his neck, while at the same time a scrawny bundle of black feathers hopped nervously away from the saddlebags. Then, opening the glove compartment of the Alvis, Kuppa removed his pistol and tranquillising darts (for which he had had to complete seventeen separate forms, documents and receipts before he was allowed to take them from Maxwell House), and began to make his way across the shifting sands of Hurghada.

---

*The well-known singer, whose recordings were the only ones stocked in the Sotnot-Re Phonograph Shop in Gurna, due to an unspoken passion of the shop's owner, Norman Sotnot-Re.

MOIST-FREE METROPOLIS

FOR A LONG TIME they were dragged in the seaweed nets down the steep bank on the other side of the channel. Their abductors were striding with eager zest, or so it seemed to Jim, whose ear was very close to the gravel-crunching foot of one abductor.

The only noises he could hear were the drag of gravel and the seaweed nets, punctuated by the occasional squawk from Doris and snort from Brenda as they rolled against certain uncomfortable patches of rough terrain. Gradually these noises became less and less, as the roughness of the descent began to ease off. After fifteen minutes of further dragging, the floor became smoother, until it had the well-worn texture of old linoleum.

On this surface, Cairo Jim was able to roll himself around a bit inside the net, until he could position himself curled upon his back, in a position not unlike an inverted tortoise. Now his face was away from the ground, and by turning his head he was able to glimpse – just – Doris in her net on his right side and Brenda in hers on his left. They did not look too badly shaken.

"Doris," he whispered in a hiss. "My dear, are you all right?"

"Rark," was all Doris could say.

 **110**

He turned his head the other way. "And you, Brenda, my lovely?"

"Quaaoooo," snorted the Wonder Camel, and, for the first time since he had known her, he could sense fear rushing through her nostrils.

"Keep your beak and snout up, both of you," said Jim in his best stoic tone, and he would have continued, but one of their abductors turned and looked down at him.

"Hush thy gills," the abductor said, in a voice that seemed to be coming from the depths of his stomach. "Keep thy silence until we reach the athenaeum."

Jim's heart twitched. Had he heard correctly? The *athenaeum*? He quickly recalled that in ancient Greece this had been the name of the temple at Athena where poets and other such types often met. Was it possible there was a similar meeting place here? Was it possible that, through his silvery cocoon-like covering, they were able to discern that *he* had poetic tendencies?

They came to the bottom of the slope, and all three of the abductors dragged their netted captives around a corner and continued along a street, much narrower than the bank down which they had been pulled, but still wide enough for four chariots to hurtle down, side by side.

Now, for the first time, Jim was able to gain a proper, unobscured view of these beings who were doing all the pulling. They were not especially tall, and had very thick arms and legs, from which tiny, feathery follicles sprouted like ferns in a rainforest. Jim squinted hard at these strange sproutings, trying to determine what

exactly they were. They didn't quite resemble hairs; they were too curly, and seemed to waft around a lot, as though they all had a life of their own, each and every one of them. They looked more like minuscule *fins* than hairs, Jim thought. Then he noticed something else, and his heart skipped a beat: where their fingers joined close to their hands, he saw small webs of skin!

Each of the beings was dressed in a short tunic of straw-coloured fabric which appeared to be rough and scratchy (almost, thought Jim, the same as the osnaburg handkerchiefs used all the time by Mrs Amun-Ra). These tunics were trimmed with bright greenish-gold braid that covered the hem lines and sleeve and neck openings. A simple copper dagger was held in place around the waist of each being's tunic by a coarse rope belt, tied above the centre of the stomach.

Two of the abductors were talking quietly to each other in low, mumbling tones, and their heads were turned towards each other. Jim was looking almost straight up into their faces, and his heart skipped another beat.

Instead of eyebrows, two pairs of flat, thin fins grew along the ridges at the bottoms of these beings' foreheads. Like the feathery follicles sprouting from their arms, these fin-eyebrows seemed to have lives of their own, and they moved silently about, backwards and forwards, bristling to the front and then lying flat again. It was as though they were acting like miniature antennae on the faces of the creatures.

Jim watched their mouths carefully as they conversed,

but he couldn't hear precisely what they were saying to each other. Nor could he lip-read from their mouths, for they were not formed in the same shape as an above-ground being's: they were essentially a perfect "O" shape, which never closed, as opposed to Jim's lips which were capable of a wide assortment of different shapes, and which he always kept closed when he wasn't speaking, or in between mouthfuls of food.

Jim's, Doris's and Brenda's belts were going berserk: flashing and beeping and bipping and throwing out beams of halogen light as though the panic of the heavens had got into them. Doris, her wing pinioned uncomfortably above her head and her beak stuck very close to her belly, could not help observing that it was now four thirty-seven in Helsinki.

On and on the captors dragged them, without regard for their comfort or positions. By a bit of careful wriggling, Jim was able to turn himself so that he was slightly on his side, with his face very close to the rough seaweed of the netting. Through the holes in the weave he watched as the city moved slowly, jerkingly past him.

To the left he could see a vast curved wall with a huge opened gate. As he was pulled past this gate he glimpsed, only for a few moments, some vehicles blurring past. Chariots, he thought excitedly. Of course! This was the hippodrome, and there was some sort of race in progress.

The hippodrome was soon behind them. Jim pushed his face closer to the netting to see what was coming up next. Ahead, through the thick, sprouting legs of the

 **113**

abductor in front of him, the archaeologist-poet could see that they had arrived at a wide, open courtyard. At the far end was a high series of steps, crowned with a row of cylindrical columns. Some of the columns were intact, but others had been broken at various points on their trunks, cut through as a knife would a candle. Even though they were not as they had presumably once been, they still towered taller than half-a-dozen men standing on each other's shoulders, and were too thick for several people to join hands around.

One of the captors turned to the others. From his rounded mouth came a single grunt. They all stopped and grunted back.

"What's happening?" whispered Doris. "Why've we stopped?"

Jim turned his shoulder so that he could see her and Brenda. "It looks like some sort of meeting place. Maybe it's the city's forum."

"Quaaooo," wriggled Brenda.

One of the beings turned a hostile face. "Quell thy loud thoughts," he commanded.

Doris tried to flap her wings to let him know who was boss, but of course she was helpless. The beings muttered amongst themselves for a while, and then one of their number nodded and sped off towards a doorway in the wall at the far end of the space. He disappeared through the doorway, and several minutes later he returned with a large bronze key in his hand. This he waved aloft at his comrades.

"Athenaeum," he declared, and there followed a chorus of the word from all the others. At the end of it they all laughed, and some – those who were not holding the nets – even clapped their hands, and stomped their feet on the rough stones.

With no more ado, they dragged Jim, Doris and Brenda across the cobbled courtyard, in the direction of the steps and the columns. When they reached the steps, one of the creatures hoisted Jim (still in his net) over his shoulder, one hoisted Doris (in her net) under his arm, and four of them lifted Brenda onto their shoulders, pall-bearer style. Then, with a quick spring, they all bounded up the huge flight of steps.

The being with the bronze key led the way, and inserted the key into the lock of a heavy wooden door. There was a rattling, and a bit of turning, and the being placed his shoulder heavily and forcefully against the door. It opened with a screech so loud it should have been heard on the earth's surface, far, far above.

The beings lowered their netted catches to the floor. With deft handiwork they removed the nets and shoved Jim, Doris and Brenda into the gloom ahead.

"Keeper of the Sacrarium will inspect thou hence," announced one of the beings solemnly.

Jim opened his mouth to ask a question, but before he could utter a syllable, the beings had trundled out of the door, slamming it shut and locking it securely behind them.

IN THE GLOOMY ATHENAEUM

FOR SEVERAL MINUTES neither Jim, Doris nor Brenda made any noise or movement as their eyes became accustomed to the dimness, which was as chilling as any they'd ever known.

Gradually there became visible, at various points mid-way up the walls, small, pointed, shoe-shaped lamps, made from terracotta and set into alcoves. These lamps were all lit, and their glimmering amber flames, shooting flickering, haphazard spears of light up onto the plaster walls, provided the only means of illumination in this, the trio's new-found prison.

Then Doris spoke up, her harsh squawk jarring the eerie silence. "If this is their idea of hospitality, you can plonk me on a stick and call me Tallulah. Rerk!"

Brenda, thankful that her small feathered amigo had broken the stillness, snorted nervously.

"Goodness," muttered Jim. "I always imagined that an athenaeum would be a much more – *genteel* sort of place. Better decorated, I suppose, with prints on the walls in big gold frames, and lots of books and parchment paper and quills, and low tables for the poets to work on. This looks more like a dungeon."

It certainly did. Now their eyes were fully used to the

low lighting, and they were able to see much more of their surroundings. They were in a long, wide room, the height of which was very hard to determine on account of the lamplight's not reaching very high up the walls. These were a drab rusty colour, and here and there they were covered in darker patches with wishy-washy borders – similar to patches of rising damp Cairo Jim had often noticed on certain walls in the Old Relics Society.

In the corners at both ends of the room stood four fat, round pillars, disappearing up into the darkness. Each of these pillars was as wide as a two-thousand year old sequoia tree, and probably just as ancient: in places, their plaster coatings had flaked and fallen away to reveal their fine brickwork. At the far end of the athenaeum, there was very little room between the two columns, much less than at the end where the trio stood, and it occurred to Jim that the room was tapered, and that they were standing at the wider end.

Along both of the side walls ran two broad benches, made of some kind of rock. They were perfectly flat on the tops and had ornately carved pedestals underneath. Doris waddled over to one of these and had a bit of a poke around with her beak. "Hmm," she announced, "they're fashioned after the paw of a lion. A bit rough, though. Slightly crude for my tastes, but then we're not exactly in a position to be able to choose our furnishings, are we?"

In front of the pillars at the opposite end there was another bench, set at right angles to those that ran along

the side walls. This bench was the same as the others except in length; it was shorter, and appeared because of this to be altogether chunkier. On each end of this bench burned another two shoe-shaped lamps.

"Jim," said Doris, remembering what one of their captors had said before he had shut them in, "what's a 'Sacrarium'?"

"It's a place – er – it's where—" He scratched his chin impatiently, trying to remember. "Never mind about that now, my dear. The first thing we have to do is look for a means of escape."

He removed his damp pith helmet, then his cranium cover, and donned his pith helmet again. "That's better," he breathed heavily. "It was getting awfully hot in there."

"Good idea," said Doris. She tugged at the zip on her own silver suit.

"Brenda, my lovely, you go down to the pillars at the far end. Try and sniff out any break in the wall behind them – any sort of opening that may have been covered over."

"Quaaooo!" The Wonder Camel began making her way to the far end.

"Doris, my dear, you take the wall to your right. Flutter up and down if you can, but mind out for cobwebs. We don't want you getting your wings fairy-flossed like that time in the tomb of Queen Neferonasunday."

"Rerark! It couldn't happen twice." She stepped out of the suit and kicked it underneath the bench nearest

her. A few of her beautiful gold-and-blue feathers, unstuck from the rough dragging she had been through, spilled forlornly from the discarded suit to the floor.

"And I'll have a go at this door. Let's see—" He ran his hands flat along the wood, pushing as hard as he could. "Hmm. Solid as a rock. No rot in *this*."

"*Quaaaaaooooo!*"

"What the—?" started Jim, wheeling around in Brenda's direction.

"Praaark!" Doris, too, jumped almost out of her feathers and turned to see what had upset her friend.

Brenda was rearing up onto her hind legs, the hairs on her humps standing on end underneath her silver suit. Her nostrils were flaring and her eyes glaring wildly at the pillar in the left-hand corner.

"QUAAAOOO!"

"Brenda, what's the matter?" cried the macaw.

"Look, Doris, there's your answer! Steady on, my lovely," soothed Jim. He dashed to Brenda's side and put his arm around her thick neck. Then, with careful, trusting force, he brought her frontal portions down to the ground. When he had her calm again he led her as far away from the pillar as he could.

The cause for Brenda's alarm continued to waft out from behind the pillar: a thick, gungy column of foul-smelling smoke. It blew sideways, and then broke up into a pattern similar to the most dainty of maidenhair ferns, all delicate and hesitant and greyish-brown, before rising straight up to mingle with the gloom at the top of the

 **119**

athenaeum. Then a new bout of this foul smoke came, blasting out from behind the pillar with the same arrogant huffiness, and the whole dissolving process happened again.

Doris looked at Jim. "K–k–k–kuppa?" she whispered. "All the way down here?"

Cairo Jim's heart beat in his chest like a tom-tom in the jungle. He tried to answer her, but the inside of his mouth had gone instantaneously dry, and he was unable to make any sort of noise at all. All he could do was shrug his shoulders and perspire.

"I don't suppose," came a low, grunting rumble of a voice from behind the pillar, "that any of you lot have happened to behold a golden *sarcophagus* on your way here? Arrrrr."

Into the dim lamplight, the owner of the voice slowly emerged. Looking a little worse for wear, Neptune Bone squeezed through the space between the two pillars and stood defiantly before them, his fleshy hands clutching the hem of his emerald-green waistcoat, his abhorrently ponging cigar clenched between his teeth. Behind him, in a jumbled pile on the floor, lay his diving suit and helmet. "How nice of you all to drop in," he sneered sarcastically. "If I'd known you were coming I'd have baked a cake. Arrrr."

"Rark!" squawked Doris.

"Quaoo," snorted Brenda, less tense than she had been.

Overcome with shock and relief, Cairo Jim rushed to

Bone and extended his hand. "Bone!" he gasped. "Thank Zeus you're alive."

Bone took the cigar from his mouth and looked down his wide nose at Jim's hand. "If you don't altogether mind," he snorted, "I won't shake with you. I've only just manicured."

Jim withdrew his hand and used it to adjust his pith helmet. "We've been terribly worried about you."

"*We?*"

"Desdemona's very upset, you know. When last we saw her she was lamenting fit to burst."

"That flying flapdoodler? Those plumes of doom? Why should she be upset? The raucous repository of rancidness, why on earth—?"

"Precisely," Cairo Jim interrupted. "She's on the earth, and you're under the sea. You're her friend, Bone. Whether you like it or not, she misses you."

"Hmmph." The larger archaeologist puffed again on his cigar as he went and sat on the shorter bench. "And what about Mustafa Kuppa?" he sneered. "He hasn't managed to get hold of her yet, has he?"

"I have no idea," replied Jim. "Don't worry, I didn't give away your location."

"*How decent* of you." Bone's voiced dripped with snideness. "By the way, did you know your brass ring is dangling? And that you look outrageous in that suit, like an addled escapee from a Busby Berkeley musical film. Soon you'll all be lying on the floor and making strange shapes with your arms and legs, I suppose."

Jim sat on one of the wall benches and took off his pith helmet, and Doris fluttered over to join him. (She had been helping Brenda unzip her diving suit, while the both of them had been listening intently to the two humans.) "So," he addressed Bone, "they captured you as well?"

"Aaarrr. Blasted luck that was. I don't know how such a thing could've occurred to someone as quick-thinking as myself. Most unexpected. There I was, perusing the lower depths for old Savlon's doub— Er, for my personal pleasure, when suddenly, in the darkness behind me, I saw the coral bend and sway. Not gently, you understand, but with a *force* behind it. Altogether unnatural and ominous. I stopped and watched, and then those plankton men came at me. Brutes!"

"Plankton men?" said Doris.

"I think your feathered handbag made a noise," Bone said to Jim. "Yes, plankton men. This is my second night down here, and I've had time to learn a little bit about the place. Inquisitiveness is a natural trait in us geniuses. I pretended to make friends with the creature who comes in and feeds me – he's a bit on the dull side, and never shuts his mouth, but he likes to have a chat – and I have learned much. Tyrone, I call him, as he reminds me of that actor in the fillums, although the interior of *his* gullet was on display far less, that's for certain. Well, Tyrone said that those thugs who snatched me – and presumably you lot as well – are the plankton men. They go out in squads every six hours or so and

collect plankton in those dreadfully uncomfortable nets. Apparently the people in this sunken civilisation scoff the stuff."

"The plankton men are like our fishermen?" suggested Jim.

"That's what I said to Tyrone, but he said no. You see, they also have designated beings down here whose job it is to collect fish. Fish is apparently the staple diet of these people – er, creatures, and plankton is considered a *delicacy*. So Tyrone says. I imagine it's sort of like their version of our caviar, a plate of which I would dearly love to consume right at this moment. It is entirely more delicious than plankton, which tastes, I imagine, like garden weeds that have matured inside one of Mrs Amun-Ra's boots in the sun for a fortnight."

"That's enough about Mrs Amun-Ra," Jim said quickly.

"Arr, I'm so sorry. You're very big on this *friends* thing, aren't you?"

Jim chose to ignore the rudeness. "What happened when they netted you?" he asked.

Bone paused to blow a heavy ring of smoke towards the far wall. "Arrr. They threw that confounded net at me and trussed me up like a bird about to go into the oven."

"*Reerarrkk!*" screeched Doris, and Jim reached out and patted her crest.

"Then they dragged me up that colossal channel and past the waterline. At the top, in the watertight region, they stopped to tell a joke or something – I couldn't

understand what they were gabbling about. While they were yapping, I managed to get m'deluxe waterproof fez with the drip-dry tassel off m'diving helmet, and scribbled a message into it with the waterproof crayon I'd packed with m'cigars and manicure kit. Then, ensuring that the thugs weren't watching, I reached down through the gaps in the net and grabbed up a handful of rocks. I put the rocks into the fez, squeezed the lot through the net, and carefully flung it down into the water, hoping it would sink."

"It did," said Jim. "Then it found its way to the surface, and Desdemona got it. That's why we're here."

Bone said nothing at this comment, preferring to signal his disdain by screwing up his nose as though he had just smelled a disagreeable odour. He took a puff on his shortening cigar, flicked the ash in Brenda's general direction, and continued his tale:

"Then they pulled me rather humiliatingly through the town and we arrived, after much bruising of my tender pores, at this place." He looked around wearily. "You needn't think about escaping, you know; the first thing I did was scour every nook and cranny for an exit. Chipped three fingernails in the process, blast it. There's no way out. We're imprisoned, square and simple. I am" – and he let out a hopeless sigh, his flabby shoulders sagging in the process – "incarcerated with imbeciles. Confined with Cairo Jim. Now *there's* a chapter for my memoirs. Not that they matter any more; I'll never

get out of here to write even a shopping list."

He took a last drag on the cigar and slowly stubbed it out on the top of the bench. "That was the last of those, as well. Oh, I always imagined that Doom would be altogether more *fun* than this. What a wretched way to go. And high up above, those I have known, those who have had the good taste to worship me, will sit upon the ground and tell sad tales of the death of Bone— Aaaaarrrr!"

Doris cringed at his misappropriation of Shakespeare's words.

"What do you think they're going to do with us?" Jim asked quietly.

"I have no idea," Bone grunted. He ran his fingers through his beard. Doris noticed that his hands were sweating and trembling slightly.

"What have they done to you since you've been in here?"

"Fed me. Fed me and fed me and fed me. Up to m'eyeballs with food. Now ordinarily, I'd have no objections to that, but there's only so much plankton and fish a genius can take. The metabolism of a man such as myself craves the finer things, it's only natural."

"Is that all they've done?"

"Incessant torture of victuals! Arrr. Tyrone comes in here practically every half an hour with those ridiculous little platters piled high with the stuff." He jerked his thumb at the corner, and Jim, Doris and Brenda looked. In a pile lay ten or so tarnished brass plates, all of them

circular, with a small pattern inlaid into the centre of each. All of the plates were empty. "He makes sure I've eaten every last scrap. Says if I don't, I'll get the sand torture."

"Sand torture?"

"Mmm. Tyrone says they tie you down – those thugs, I imagine, they have a *flair* for brutality – and then they sprinkle scorching sand slowly into your exposed navel. It's supposed to be excruciating. Tyrone knew of someone who had it done to him, and this man – a fishman – had dreadful problems afterwards, especially when an unexpected breeze blew in his direction. He almost turned inside-out on those occasions. But Tyrone says the women found him fun to dance with, especially when it was a poussette." He wiggled his eyebrows knowingly.

"Why ever would they keep feeding you like that?"

"I think," said Bone, cracking his knuckles loudly (making Doris cringe again), "they are trying to fatten me up. Arr."

"Since when did you need help with that?" Doris squawked, and Bone shot her a filthy glare.

"Doris," whispered Jim. "Don't sink to his level."

"I shall choose to ignore the comments of your burlesqued beaked basket, Jim. My satisfaction will come knowing that her situation is as desperate as mine: unutterably wretched. As I was explaining, I think they are trying to fatten me up. There is a little particularity that occurred shortly after I was incarcerated here, which convinces me of the matter. A very tall fishwoman came in and with a long implement poked me all about, taking

my measurements. Another fishwoman, a real prawn face who took an instant dislike to me for some reason, stood in the background and scribbled down the measurements. Then, after some minutes of these ruthless intrusions, they left."

Brenda gave a snort, wishing she had her western adventure novel with her right now.

"Who were they?" asked Jim.

Bone passed his index finger close to the flame in the lamp nearest him. "Tyrone told me later that the tall one is Celestera, the Keeper of the Sacrarium, and the sourpuss is her maiden-of-honour. Whatever that means for me, I don't know."

The word "Sacrarium" wafted around the inside of Jim's head, like a telephone call from an old familiar friend he hadn't seen in years. That word he had heard often at one stage in his life when he was a younger man, but he couldn't now for the life of him remember what it meant. What in the name of Nespernub was a Sacrarium?

He put the thought on hold and looked again at Bone. "One thing I need to know: you're down here because of *Sekheret*, aren't you?"

Bone gave his most cringe-making smirk. "There's no hope of finding him now. The only thing we'll find is eternal slavery at best, and" – he lowered his deep voice – "a forgotten, submerged ending. We're going to Hell in a fez-box. What a way to shuffle off! Arrr."

Jim shook his head. "I never would have given you

credit for it, Bone. There are surely less dangerous relics to look for. I really underestimated you.

"How do you mean?"

"I never thought you were so brave. For goodness' sake, to risk life and whiskers like you have, all for the sake of a single sarcophagus—"

Captain Neptune Flannelbottom Bone's smirk broadened into a wide, fleshy-lipped grin. He thought of the doubloons of Sir Murray Savlon, and his beard tingled at the image of all that alluring gold. He threw back his head and laughed – a high-pitched, hysterical roar that bounced off the walls and all around the tranquil gloom of the athenaeum.

"Raark!" squawked Doris. "He's gone loony!"

"Bone, what's the matter? What's so amusing?"

Bone managed to control his outburst until only his waistcoated paunch was quivering. He looked once again at Jim and Doris, the tears still coursing down his cheeks and into his beard.

"Matter?" he half-giggled and half-snarled. "Matter? *You're* the matter. You and your silly innocence. How can you be so *naive*? How can you go and keep surviving through this great disgusting maze the philosophers call Life when you have so little gumption? Don't you realise that *nothing* is ever as it seems? That there is always an underlying reason behind every person's action in this boiling vat of putrescence which is otherwise known as Humanity? Arrr."

He stood and began pacing up and down the middle

of the floor. "How can you be so trusting? How, in the name of Medusa, can you be so – *good*? There is always an ulterior motive; *things are never what they seem*! I came after the sarcophagus of Sekheret, you're quite correct."

With the swiftness of an obese panther he swivelled on his heel and faced Jim and Doris, his bottom perilously close to Brenda's snout. "But there was more to it than that, much more. You know as well as your own name, there is an overabundance of ancient coffins all through this land. Another old bit of relicania wouldn't generate much interest, and certainly not anywhere near enough glory as I seek. No, it's altogether too small a quest for someone the likes of me. Why, it'd just be put on show in the Cairo Museum, and the discoverer would get his picture in the newspapers for a day or two, and then after a year or so, when enough Museum dust had settled upon the casket lid for everyone to forget about the achievement and not even be able to recognise the casket underneath, the whole episode would become another statistic, another pathetic memory in the vast and never-ending continuum of our ridiculous profession, Archaeology. A *single sarcophagus* – he almost spat the words – "a single sarcophagus is more up your alleyway, I'd say. I was after something *much* more precious."

"Like what?" asked Jim.

Bone shut his eyes and whispered, not to Jim, Doris or Brenda, but to himself. "Mag–nif–i–cence. Aaaaaaaarrrr."

The concept dripped from his lips as though it was honey.

"He *has* gone off the twig," prerked Doris.

Bone's eyes flashed open, and he was about to utter the word *doubloons* in a forceful, fruity tone, when there was a heavy noise of a key turning in the lock of the door, and the hinges screeched like a thousand tormented souls howling up a wind shaft.

A MYSTERIOUS PROD

AS ONE, Jim, Doris, Brenda and Bone fell silent, their attention fixed singularly upon the door as it opened towards them.

Outside, in the constant lamp-and-candle-light of the city, they could see two thuggish figures, squat and finny, standing on either side of the doorway. They were both looking at each other with grim expressions, and one of them was swinging the huge brass key on his chain. Neither of the beings made any sound at all.

Then, completely unannounced, a smaller figure came rushing through the middle of them, carrying no less than eight plates full of grey-coloured, squishy matter in his hands and balanced in the crooks of his elbows and upon his shoulders and his head. The eighth plate was being held by its rim in between his teeth, and this put a strange, strained smile on his face, which seemed at odds with the strenuous and difficult task he was at that moment performing.

"This is Tyrone," Bone announced. "Chatterbox that he is."

As soon as Tyrone was well within the walls of the athenaeum, the two thuggish figures grunted to each other and swiftly closed the door with another ghastly

screech. Tyrone squatted and carefully began to place his plates onto the nearest bench. He wore the same kind of bordered, straw-coloured tunic as every other native Atlantean, although it seemed much more becoming on his more slender frame than on the plankton men.

Jim watched him as he deftly deposited the plates, and could not help comparing his movements to papyrus stalks being wafted in the breeze.

As soon as Tyrone had laid down the last plate, he turned to face them. His eyes were positively bright as his gaze wandered across the forms of Doris and Brenda (now completely divested of their silver suits), to Jim.

Bone stepped forward. "Aaarr. Have you brought me more of that muck?" he growled.

"Oh, Magnificent Genius Bone—" said Tyrone.

("I told him that was my name," Bone whispered to Jim.)

"—yea, I have brought thee more of the feastiverous fare thou desires. Also there is a generous share for thy newly arrived companions. They must eat, and digest, and all will be well."

"Well for what?" asked Cairo Jim, and Doris fluttered her wings anxiously.

Tyrone turned his head away from Jim's eye. "I must not speak at length to thee. I have already been talked to most sternly for saying such vasty amounts of words to my friend, Magnificent Genius Bone. I should not continue my verbal commerce at great length, I have been warned."

He looked again at them, and his voice dropped to a point just above a low whisper. "If I speak with excess to thee, I will be strapped down and given the sand torture. That I could not bear. I am, after all, a gentle Atlantean, not given to violence of any manner. I can hardly bear to clip the nails at the ends of my fingers, such does it upset me to hear the suddenness of the clippers as they snap together with their fierce animosity." He sighed deeply, and Brenda was sure she saw him shudder slightly beneath his tunic.

Jim took a step closer to this willowy being and spoke with calm authority, even though his ribcage was tingling with a multitude of hitherto unknown fears. "Please, sir, would you tell us what is our intended fate? What do your people plan to do with us?"

Bone snarled and pushed Jim aside. "I'll do the talking here, if you don't mind."

"Quaaoo!"

"It's all right, Brenda, we'll let Captain Bone talk."

"You bet your dicky-bird we will," Bone snorted. He turned to Tyrone. "So, my friend, tell us: what *is* our intended fate? What do you lot plan to do with us? Come on, pipe up! Give us your usual onslaught of eloquence."

Tyrone began hopping up and down in his leather sandals. "Oh, Magnificent Genius Bone, this is such an exciting afternoon for all Atlanteans. Immensely, incalculably exciting. But it is nothing in comparison to what will happen *tomorrow*."

"Tomorrow?" growled Bone.

"Tomorrow?" said Jim.

"Tomorrow? Rerk."

"Quaaooo?"

"I must not tarry here," Tyrone muttered. "Why, if I were caught here when she comes, it would be the hot sand for absolute certain!"

"Who's she?" Jim asked, frowning.

"Why, the Keeper of the Sacrarium, of course. She herself. You remember, oh Magnificent Genius Bone, she came to thee on yesterday's evening. She is paying all of thee another visit this very afternoon!" He made the announcement in the kind of hushed reverence one usually uses to announce an event of the most supreme importance.

"The Keeper of the Sacrarium?" asked Jim. "What does she want with us?"

Tyrone's eyes became glassy, and his eyebrow fins swayed as though they were oscillating backwards and forwards. "She is coming for the Great Inspection, which, because of her exalted office, she must of course carry out. She will – oh, by the Gods, no! I must make myself scarce, otherwise—"

The dreadful screeching shot into the athenaeum like a strangulated cannon's volley, and the door began to open. Tyrone half-wafted, half-raced to the far end of the room, where he quickly ducked through the space between the two pillars and concealed himself behind one of them.

Doris hopped across to Brenda and nuzzled into the warm cleft between her humps, a position from where

she could see everything but not be seen too prominently herself.

Through the open doorway, two sturdy Atlanteans brushed past the guards. They swiftly entered the athenaeum and stood on each side of the door, facing the centre of the room. Both of them wore salmon-coloured tunics, open at the sides and fastened at a small point near their hips with a piece of stout rope.

From beneath the tunics they each deftly produced an uncommonly long trumpet, fashioned (it seemed to Jim) from long, tapered shells with several holes drilled in them. The two sturdy creatures raised these trumpets to their open mouths and blew, their cheeks puffing out, their eyes bulging, and their eyebrow-fins waving about in all directions.

The noise blared into the room and bounced off the walls and columns.

Bone rolled his eyes and muttered under his breath. "Arrrr, they did that last time. Pomp-and-ceremony mongers!"

The trumpeters lowered their instruments and held them by their sides. A few seconds passed, Jim's ears ringing and Brenda's earflaps tingling, and then a female Atlantean, short and dumpy and holding a flat piece of stone tablet and a writing implement similar to a thick pencil, stepped into the doorway.

She gazed down into the room at the captives and in a cold, hard voice, announced the arrival of her mistress:

"Thou shall be honoured to receive the Keeper of the Most Holy Sacrarium, the Guardian of the Offeratory, the Chief High Preparer, the Honourable Patroness, Celestera."

The two trumpeters sank to their knees, and the dumpy woman stepped inside the room before she, too, sank to her knees.

Bone prodded Jim in the back. "You'd better do likewise," he hissed. "These clodhopping cousins of calamari expect it." And with a heavy grunt, he knelt, followed closely by Jim.

Now a small glow of light appeared on the other side of the door. It grew brighter and brighter as it came closer and closer, and very soon it was as bright as the light coming from twenty candles, which wasn't surprising, as that was exactly what was causing it.

Into the athenaeum swept a tall, willowy female Atlantean, and upon this woman's tightly curled hair sat an ornate and intricate candelabra that rose up from the top of her head in the shape of a well-pruned Christmas tree. The twenty fat candles were sitting in small shoe-shaped sconces which had been crafted into the towering headdress, and their flickering flames cast the kind of mellow light upon her face that Inspector Mustafa Kuppa was always dreaming about.

The tall female looked down at Bone. Her nose wrinkled and she shifted her inspection to Jim, Doris and Brenda. Now her eyes lit up. She reached to her shoulder, where a bright yellow clam shell was attached

to her heavy green robe. With a twist of her webbed hand she removed the shell, and her robe fell open to reveal a glittering gown with more pleats than Jim had ever seen, even on anything his friend Jocelyn Osgood had worn when they had cause to socialise in the evenings at certain Cairo nightclubs. In between each of the pleats, many tiny seahorses were clinging, swaying back and forth every time the glittering fabric rolled with her movements.

"Nice frock," said Bone, and Celestera's maiden-of-honour looked up and hissed a loud *Shh*! at him.

The candle-lit Celestera turned her head to the kneeling woman. "Glorious, these are the creatures who rained down upon us?" she asked in a voice like rolling thunder.

"They are, wise Celestera."

Celestera looked upon Jim, and extended her hand to point at him. "Rise, thou gift from above," she commanded.

With trembling thighs, Jim obeyed.

"Didst all of thee travel to this land in this apparel?" There was a tone of annoyance in her voice. "Or hast thee other attire?"

Jim thought for a moment about what she had asked, then he gestured to the pile of silver fabric lying on the floor: his silver cranium cover with the built-in goggles, and Doris's and Brenda's outfits. "We were wearing those when we were waylaid," he answered.

Celestera turned her head slowly, the weight of her

candles making quicker movement impossible. She saw the pile of crumpled silver material and her eyes narrowed into pleased slits. She slowly turned her head to what sat next to the material. When her eyes focused on Brenda, with Doris nestled between her humps, her opened, rounded mouth let out an involuntary gasp.

"What kind of manna is this? A beast the size of this? With another beast with such bright hues sprouting from the valley in her back?"

"She's a feathered wart," blurted Bone, and Glorious told him to *Shh*! again, this time much more loudly.

"That is Brenda," answered Jim. "She's my friend. And on her back is my other dear friend, Doris. She's completely detachable. Come here, my dear."

Doris gave a tiny preerk and, with her eyes fixed firmly on Celestera, flew tentatively to Jim and settled on his outstretched arm.

"By the Greatest of Equinoxes," Celestera whispered. "This is surely the most generous fortune to arrive here in Atlantis in living memory. First, the big one with the smoking mouth and bristly gills." She turned her head slowly to Bone. "Not fully suitable for our needs tomorrow, a poor specimen to say the least, but better than the absence of anything. But now, now, we have been blessed indeed! Another one, bristle-less, has arrived, who has brought us one the size of four with hills and valleys, and a small one that can swim through air."

She looked at Glorious. "In times to come they will attribute this great bounty to Celestera. No future

Keeper of the Sacrarium could ever match this collection!"

"Most certainly not, Noble Celestera."

"Collection?" Jim whispered to Bone. "What does she mean?"

"Maybe she's going to shrivel us down and hang us from that ostentatious outfit she's wearing," Bone sneered. "I bet all those seahorses take some cleaning, otherwise the pong—"

"SHH!" shhed Glorious.

Celestera cast out her hand in the direction of her maiden-of-honour. "Rise, Glorious, and let us take the dimensions of our new gains. Especially the hilled-and-valleyed one."

From one of the heavy folds in her gown, she took out two long, straight pieces of coral, bright pink and worn smooth. Both pieces were joined at one end by some seaweedy twine. As Celestera held them up towards the light streaming from her candle-addled head, Jim observed that there were small marks painted at regular intervals onto them.

"Ask the golden one to stand," Celestera commanded Jim.

He frowned at her bossiness, but glimpsed the burly trumpeters at the door and did as he was told.

"Brenda, my lovely, please stand for a few moments."

"Quaaoo?" Her eyelashes trembled as she looked uncertainly at her friend.

"Don't worry, I won't let anything nasty happen."

The Wonder Camel's hair bristled reassuringly from the sincerity in his voice and she slowly rose. When she had reached her full height, both Celestera and Glorious gasped loudly. Even the trumpeters' mouths opened wider than they had previously been.

"By Hera!" Celestera exclaimed. "She is surely what we have lost these many years!"

"Eh?" Bone muttered.

"Sh!" hissed Glorious.

"Prawn features," he thought contemptuously.

"Rark!" Doris whispered to Jim. "Lost? What does she mean?"

"I wish I knew," he whispered back.

Without another word, Celestera glided slowly over to Brenda, and proceeded to measure her all over. Each and every hump, bump, cavity, nostril, kneecap, hoof and eyelash hair was touched lightly by the two pieces of marked coral. Whenever Celestera had finished inspecting a particular feature or area, she would pronounce some strange-sounding words to Glorious, who would then scratch something with her writing implement onto the stone tablet she had resting on her arm.

"Arr," Bone said behind his hand to Jim. "They did this to me first. It was just like being welcomed into one of those dieting clubs, not that I'd know first-hand, of course, a woman I knew—"

"Desist thy drivellings!" Glorious warned between recording measurements.

"Pretzel-face," Bone scowled.

Eventually they finished measuring Brenda, and Celestera's wide opened mouth took on a different shape. It remained fully opened, but the corners became slightly straighter, almost as if she were smiling.

"Thy measurements tally very closely with thy forebears. They who have stayed away for so long. Now," she announced, "for the one who swims through air."

In the same way, Doris was also measured as she sat on Jim's crooked arm.

When they had recorded everything to their satisfaction, Celestera nodded and Glorious lowered her writing implement and kneeled once more. The candle-lit Keeper of the Sacrarium bowed her head to the captives, her flames coming near to their faces. When she looked up again, her eyes fixed on Brenda and she made a strange sound with her tongue against the roof of her mouth.

Then she turned and glided majestically out of the athenaeum, plunging it back into the gloom by which it was normally impregnated.

When she had gone, Glorious stood and addressed them. "Thou will be ready on the morrow, early. Thy Keeper and Feeder will awaken thee at the appropriate hour for dressing. It is of vital importance that adornment is the same as when thou arrived at Atlantis."

To Jim, she added, "Ensure that the hilled-and-valleyed one eats the entire portion of the food that has been granted this evening. Hers is the greatest need."

She placed her stone tablet under her arm and

looked coolly at them. "Thy fortune is to be envied. It is a rare occasion to be present at the Grand Equinox of Glisteneratum!"

"The Grand *what*?" asked Cairo Jim.

Glorious was marching for the door. "You will know more on the morrow's morn."

"Wait!" cried Bone, grunting to his feet. "What about *me*? Aren't you going to prod me with that rudimentary ruler? I was here first, let me remind you of that! I'm far more important than all of these—"

Glorious paused between the two trumpeters. She looked at Bone, then gave the trumpeters a signal. As one, they lifted their instruments to their opened mouths and pointed them at the indignant and flustered face of the bearded one. The noise exploded into his face, parting the hairs in the middle of his moustache and making his ears ring like bells.

"I think she said 'shh'," Doris squawked, as Glorious and the trumpeters left the athenaeum, slamming the heavy door after them.

SLUMBER OF SINISTERNESS

CAIRO JIM'S SLEEP that night was riddled with images dredged up from somewhere he knew not.

As soon as he had bade goodnight to Doris and Brenda and Bone (who grunted something about wishing he had never laid eyes on flabellum wafters in the first place, before turning his face to the wall), and had laid down his head on the hard stone bench, he spiralled off into slumber.

The nightmare came to him quickly. Jocelyn Osgood, his Flight Attendant acquaintance from Valkyrian Airways, had flown down to him in a little biplane with a propeller sounding more like hiccuping thunder than machinery. Jim was sitting in front of the athenaeum, on the steep stone steps by the broken pillars, and Jocelyn stepped buoyantly from her cockpit, jumped from the wing of the aeroplane, and strode coolly and confidently towards him.

"Jim, Jim, why so glum?" she asked, her plum-coloured scarf waving about in the water surrounding her. For in the dream Atlantis was completely submerged.

He looked up and saw her eyes staring down at him. Somehow they were five times bigger than they should have been, and they were zesty and wild, which was most out of character for someone like Jocelyn Osgood.

 **143**

"Because," he answered, his utterance making bubbles spew out from his mouth like jet fountains, "this is it. The End. There's nothing else. We've come to where there is no more."

Jocelyn threw back her head and laughed a gurgle of watery hilarity. "The end? What ever are you babbling about? It's not the end until the sun goes down and doesn't come up again."

A dull clatter of metal on stone. It rang out as though it were being magnified through a megaphone, and Cairo Jim woke up. He blinked and peered through the dim lamplight in the athenaeum. Doris, sleeping next to Brenda and perched on the edge of the bench at the end of the room, had stirred in her sleep and had knocked the empty tarnished brass plate (empty because they had eaten the plankton and fish from it) onto Brenda's diving suit which lay crumpled on the floor. There was a flash of light as the plate glinted in the lampglow on its brief journey.

On the bench opposite, Bone snored loudly, his bulbous nose nestled into a small niche in the stone wall. Doris snuggled against Brenda's rump, rubbing her mandible sleepily into the Wonder Camel's hair.

Brenda gave a quiet snort. She too had been woken by the noise of the plate falling, but when she saw Doris snuggling against her she realised her feathered friend had been responsible for it, and so she settled herself again to sleep. As she lowered her long neck towards the

bench, her eye caught Jim's.

"It's all right, my lovely," he said quietly, his voice wavering. "Go back to sleep. I'm sure tomorrow will turn out just fine."

"Quaaoo," she snorted. She shook her head in a circle and laid it down.

Jim turned to face the wall of his prison, his blood running colder than a glacier at the prospect of the Grand Equinox of Glisteneratum to which they would awaken.

VIEW FROM THE SACRARIUM

TO INSPECTOR MUSTAFA Kuppa of the Antiquities Squad (still on his ever-alert vigil by the shores of the Red Sea), it was nothing more than a shaft of desert sunlight streaming down towards the water. (Not even mellow light, as he preferred it.)

If he had looked a little more intently through his Hollywood-style sun-spectacles at it, however, he would have observed that it was a rare light: brighter and far more intense than an ordinary shaft of sunlight, and there was something very ancient about its ray, especially at that point where it hit the water and, like a pin-prick, continued downwards, far beneath the shifting depths.

Mustafa Kuppa was sweatingly unaware, as he swatted at a noisy blowfly about to land on his aquiline nose, that soon, at a special time designated long before, this unusual shaft of illumination would hit a point at the bottom of the ocean, and its miraculous powers of ancient natural mystery would be unleashed. Miraculous powers which would contain serious repercussions for Cairo Jim, Doris, Brenda the Wonder Camel, and even for his prey, Captain Neptune Bone.

Beyond the next sand dune, a dreadful lament came from the throat of a particularly grotty raven...

▲ ▲ ▲

The door opened with the same blood-pasteurising screech which they had all experienced at least half-a-dozen times since their incarceration. Nevertheless, the sound rattled through all of their ribcages.

Tyrone rushed waftingly through the door, the muted light from the city's constantly burning lamps shimmering around his shoulders and finny ears. "Hasten, hasten," he cried. "The hour itself will soon be upon us!"

Cairo Jim sat up on the bench, blinking heavily.

Doris woke with a *rerk* and rubbed the sleep from her eyes with her wing.

"Aarr," Bone growled. He swung his legs to the floor and caressed the corners of his moustache away from his beard and out of the corners of his mouth. "What confounded hour are you talking about, you garrulous goby?"

Tyrone wrung his webbed hands. "The hour we wait for all our existences, of course. The hour that heralded the golden age, long ago."

"Golden age?" said Jim. "Whatever's that?"

Tyrone shrugged. "Ask me not; I have not an inkling. Everyone speaks of the golden age, but few are they who know it."

Brenda opened her eyes and gave a waking snort. When Tyrone heard it, he spun around to see her. A look of wonderment came across his face and lingered there for a few moments before collapsing into a sad, confused expression.

"Quaaooo?"

"I am so sorry," Tyrone said, his open mouth trembling at the top of its upper lip. Then he took on a completely different tone: "Thou will all dress with haste in the apparel worn when thou all arrived in Atlantis. Do not dally, nor make verbal commerce. Dress with the utmost alacrity, for Celestera waits for thee."

"What's she waiting for?" Bone grimaced.

"To take thee to the Sacrarium, of course. Today is the day! Now I must make my departure, lest I be admonished for loitersome behaviour."

"But—" began Jim, but he said no more as Tyrone drifted quickly from them. The door was forcefully closed by the two burly guards outside (who, Doris noticed, were dressed in particularly ornate tunics and spangly sandals and headbands with seahorses inserted into them, as opposed to their usually bland outfits).

Jim looked at his two friends. "I suppose we'd better do as he says, gang. At least it'll mean we leave this awful place."

Doris hopped from her bench to her tiny silver outfit and cranium cover with the built-in goggles and beak-peg. She gave it a kick with her claw. "What'll happen, Jim?" she asked, her voice warbling in a way not altogether birdlike.

Jim stared at her for a long time, his eyes glazed. "If I could answer that question—" he began. Then he stopped and rubbed his forehead. "Come on, my friends. There are questions that sometimes are meant to

be *un*answered. For the time being, at least." He began to don his silver cranium cover.

"You and your precious 'friends' obsession," Bone snorted, making his way to his own oversized outfit. "Hrrmmph!"

As soon as they were dressed in their diving apparel, the guards opened the doors and instructed them all to vacate the athenaeum.

The four captives emerged to see, through the row of dilapidated columns, the city lit up below them. Great torches were burning atop tall stakes on every corner of every boulevard, and hordes of people, dressed in brightly coloured tunics, gowns and other antiquated garb, were hurrying towards a building close to the athenaeum itself.

One of the guards took out a long copper sword from a silver scabbard and waved it in the direction of the crowd. "Come," he ordered, his tongue darting in and out of his perpetually open mouth, "make brisk course to the Sacrarium."

The other guard began to lead the way along the platform at the top of the steps. No sooner had he taken his first step than he was joined – from nowhere it seemed – by four other guards, all of whom carried the same broad copper swords. Jim, Doris, Brenda and Bone followed these five, and they in turn were followed by the guard who had ordered them to the Sacrarium; he himself was joined by four others. It was a sturdy convoy.

"Jim," prowked Doris as she rode on her friend's shoulder, "what's in store?"

"I don't know, my dear."

"Arrrr," grumbled Bone, carrying his huge helmet on his pudgy hip. "Blast that Sekheret. Curse that Murray Savlon. Nothing's worth all this bother, not even sixteen million pounds worth of doubloons."

"Sixteen million *what*?" whispered Jim.

"Never you mind," Bone answered maliciously. "Your string's dangling again, you know."

Jim frowned at the brass ring at the end of the string banging against his kneecap as he walked.

"Quaaaooo," snorted Brenda, as her nether hump rubbed uncomfortably against something hard inside her silver suit.

"See," Bone sneered, "it's even bothering the dumb beast."

"Rark!" Doris would have given him a quick nip on the earlobe, but the guards suddenly stopped.

Brenda, at the end of the captive group, walked snout-first into the back of Bone.

"Watch it, you Bactrian booby," he scowled.

Ahead was a huge entrance to an immense building. Hundreds of people were filing into this place, and Jim could almost taste a most definite sense of excitement hanging in the air.

"This way," ordered one of the guards. He led them to a much smaller door, well away from the huge entrance.

"Looks like the tradesman's entrance," Bone said. "Not that a *Bone* would ever use one. Arrr."

"Keep sacred silence!" hissed one of the guards.

They marched them along a small, narrow passage, dimly lit by the same sort of shoe-shaped lamps that had been burning in the athenaeum. The passage was a tight fit for Brenda; she had to breathe in deeply so that her sides didn't scrape along the walls.

Presently they came to a tall wooden door. One of the guards opened it (Doris was relieved to hear no screech this time) and ushered the four captives inside. When they were all in, he nodded reverentially to them.

"Thou will wait in the Sacrarium until thou art called. Thine honour will be long remembered."

Closing the door quickly, he left them.

Bone put his helmet down on the one stone bench that ran the length of the narrow room. "So this is the much-talked-of Sacrarium, eh? Not what I'd have expected at all. Barren, isn't it? But I suppose, after that dreadful so-called athenaeum, this is luxury. At least there's a curtain."

"I wonder what's on the other side of it," Jim said. He gently pulled aside the heavy burgundy-coloured drapes. "Well, cut my fringe and call me Cleopatra!"

"Coo," cooed Doris.

"Even I am suitably impressed," Bone said aloud.

"Quaaooo." Brenda flicked her tail up and peered over Jim's shoulder. She thought a snort, and went to the far end of the Sacrarium. Crossing her legs beneath

her, she settled herself on the end of the bench.

Beyond the drapes lay the tallest-ceilinged temple that any of them had ever seen. The walls of the cavernous space were hewn from rock, as were the mighty arches rising up into the darkness. The height of them was so great that there appeared to be a fog up there.

Bone sniffed. "Incense," he muttered. "Smell it. I'd say that's incense, wouldn't you?"

"Mmm," Jim said.

"'A very ancient and fish-like smell'," Doris squawked, quoting from *The Tempest*, and Brenda felt her nostrils itching.

People began filing in through the huge doors of the temple, towards the ornately carved benches that ran from the eastern end of the temple to the western end. Once seated, they had their backs to the heavy drapes concealing the Sacrarium. Jim watched a large group enter, and observed that as soon as they sat, they all fell into a faint sort of chanting.

"Doris, my dear, can you hear what they're saying?"

"I shall endeavour—" The macaw cocked her head towards the gap in the drapes. After a few seconds she whispered. "I can't make it out. Sounds like the one word, over and over."

"Glisteneratum," thought Brenda.

"Glisteneratum," said Jim. "Listen! That's what it sounds like."

"Glisteneratum, Glisteneratum, Glisteneratum," came a thousand low tones.

"Arr, Jim, Jim, get a load of the wallpaper!" Bone's normally beady little eyes were opened wide.

Jim peered in the direction in which Bone was pointing. At the far end of the temple, near to a raised platform with another heavy burgundy drape, the "wallpaper" was hanging. Huge, beautiful slabs of clean, white marble, carved with the most delicate and intricate scenes of dancers and hunters and warriors and gods.

"Mmmmm." Bone licked his lips.

"Such beautiful antiquity," whispered Jim.

"Antiquity, anshmiquity. Think what they'd fetch on the black market. Mmmm." He wiped the drool from his beard and squinted hard at the marbles. "Y'know, Jim, they look a bit like those other marbles Elgin swiped."

Jim's skin prickled. "Of course! Don't you remember, Bone? We studied all about it at archaeology school."

"Remember what?" (There wasn't much Bone *did* remember from their time at archaeology school so many years before, as he had spent a considerable portion of his class time out by the pyramids, selling plastic scarabs to trusting tourists.)

"All the fuss about the Parthenon marbles? Elgin took them, that's right, but the ones he sold to the British Museum in 1816 for thirty-five thousand pounds—"

"Oooh," Bone gasped, his eyes lighting up.

"—weren't the *first* ones he pulled off the walls. There was another set he took before them. Do you remember what became of those?"

"Er—"

"What?" said Doris.

Jim's eyes blazed with the sort of discovery an archaeologist dreams about. "*They were lost at sea,*" he whispered. "After a shipwreck or something. People said that they'd all been recovered from that shipwreck, but I'd always had my doubts. Now we know exactly where they've ended up."

Bone wiped the droplets of excitement from his eyebrows. "These primitives must've dragged 'em off the ocean's bottom and adorned this dump with 'em. Oh, how I could use my entrepreneurial skills on *those*—"

Jim gave Bone a despairing look and was about to admonish him, when there was a near-deafening clap of trumpeting from the far end of the temple. The notes blared, echoing off the high ceiling arches. They kept blaring for some time, and all the congregated people stopped their chanting and rose to their feet, their attention focused firmly on the curtained platform by the Parthenon marbles.

At the awful sounds of the trumpets, Doris fluttered over to Brenda and sought refuge in between her silvery humps.

Then the trumpeting ceased, and music began to play. It was lively, buoyant music, full of bells and triangles and wind instruments and drums being beaten; the sort of tune that would have ordinarily caused Cairo Jim to raise his feet high into the air and maybe even prance for a bit if he was sure there was no-one else

watching. Under different circumstances, he would have done just that.

Many of the people were nodding their open-mouthed heads in time to the music, and some were clapping their finned hands lightly together.

Now the music subsided, and from a door beneath the Parthenon marbles there emerged the brightest light that anyone in the city of Atlantis had seen for a whole year. The light bobbed as it came through the low doorway, and people at the benches close to it shielded their eyes with their hands as it moved very slowly to a position on the platform directly in front of the heavy drapes.

Jim reached into his silver suit and found his desert sun-spectacles. He donned them quickly. When his eyes became accustomed to all the illumination, he saw what it was.

The Keeper of the Sacrarium, Celestera herself, was standing beneath an even more ornate headdress than she had worn when she had visited the athenaeum. Now, instead of a mere twenty fat candles in shoe-shaped holders sprouting from her hair, there were more than seventy. It was like a small laser-induced explosion, as all of the flames glittered and twinkled off the sparkled rocks that had been sewn with the tenderest care into her magnificent sweeping gown and flowing train.

"Now *that's* a frock!" Bone gasped.

"What's all this about?" whispered Jim, puzzled more than ever.

Celestera's maiden-of-honour, Glorious, came through the door beneath the marbles and took her place beside her mistress. The glowing Keeper of the Sacrarium cast her eyes over the sea of faces before her.

"Fellow Atlanteans." Her voice rolled like clouds swirling in to drop their rain. "Welcome to the Day of Days: the Annual Equinox of Glisteneratum!"

"Glisteneratum, Glisteneratum, Glisteneratum," chanted the congregation.

"Today will be a day that will be remembered above all other Equinoxes since the Golden Age began. For today, Glisteneratum has blessed us with generous abundance. Not since the Pristine Tablets rained down from the sky" – she gestured to the Parthenon marbles at her left – "have we received such great fare. Glisteneratum will be mightily pleased with our procurement of what has rained down upon us from the skies in recent times."

"What's she babbling about?" Bone frowned.

"I see," Jim said. "It's starting to make sense. They've never written anything down."

"Eh?"

Jim turned to his fellow captive. "We were shut up in the athenaeum, weren't we? The place where written records are made and supposed to be kept. The library, the repository of all their recorded knowledge. Did you lay eyes on a book? A piece of parchment, or papyrus? On *anything* with writing on it, other than that slate they took our measurements on? *They haven't recorded their history, Bone!*"

"Rock my soul," muttered Bone.

"So it makes sense that those marbles – and presumably us – have been seen to have fallen from the *skies*. To have rained down. Why, these people have absolutely no idea what happened to their city those thousands of years ago, only a dog-eared notion, made hazy by the passing of time. To them, the sea is the sky, because they have no living memory of what it was like *before*!"

"Arrr. Listen, she's continuing."

"First, my people, the tablets were sent to us. As Keeper of the Sacrarium I was told of the time between when we received the tablets and when Glisteneratum Himself came down from the skies. It was a dark time, a long, dark time of great sadness and upheaval. We are indeed fortunate that on this very Equinox, we have been provided, for the first time in countless years, with a suitable gift from the skies! For the pleasure of the Golden One!"

"Glisteneratum, Glisteneratum, Glisteneratum," the people chorused.

Celestera and Glorious turned to face the drapes opposite the ones from which the captives peeked. "Oh, mighty Glisteneratum, we greet Thee once again!"

"Glisteneratum, Glisteneratum, Glisteneratum!"

Glorious came forward and grasped the drapes.

Celestera nodded slowly, her candles pouring fountains of wax onto the floor.

Glorious pulled back the drapes.

The people sank to their knees.

Celestera lowered her head.

Cairo Jim's mouth went as dry as sandpaper.

And Captain Neptune Bone let out a shocked grunt, staggering backwards in disbelief.

For there, standing upright and resplendent on the undraped platform, was the closed sarcophagus of Pharaoh Sekheret himself!

FATELIGHT

"OPEN IT," murmured Bone, pushing his face through the gap in the drapes. "Open it! Let me behold the splendours within!"

"Sh, Bone, keep it down." Jim pulled him back.

"But the doubloons—"

"What are you talking about? Oh, my goodness, look!"

The two archaeologists saw the congregation before them swaying, as if it were a single field of wheat stalks being gently buffeted by a forceful breeze. Back and forth the Atlanteans rocked, led in their motion by Celestera, her mass of candles sending great drops of melted wax onto the platform at the base of Sekheret's sarcophagus.

Slowly, as though a whisper was being amplified a thousand times, the gathering began its chant:

"Glisteneratum, mighty One from the skies, we offer you our finest – Glisteneratum, mighty One from the skies, we offer you our finest—"

Bone looked at Jim, and Jim at Bone. Both men's faces were etched with growing panic.

The shaft of ultra-strong sunlight speared down through the upper reaches of the Red Sea. It was gathering speed

now as it shimmered onwards towards the blacker depths, its prisms of light casting crazy reflections against the seaweed and coral and off the backs of iridescent fishes.

Below, the dark and slabbery creature who had been so alarmed by the appearance of Brenda the Wonder Camel in her silvery suit some days previously, opened its ancient, sleep-riddled eye. It looked upwards, and saw the shaft of light diving towards it. Something stirred in its soft and flumpering memory, and it recalled that the same light had visited a long time ago.

The creature gave a shudder and uncoiled its vast tail from around a tower of coral. It began to slide away, well away from the illuminated intrusion, its wide and glistening body squelching ponderously along in the way that only a Kraken can move when it is not rising like a rocket towards the surface.

The shaft of light continued its dive, lighting up the darkened depths as it went, until it hit a reed-surrounded rock – the same rock Brenda had stood on at the entrance to the enormous channel that rose up to the city. Upon this rock was a glitteringly smooth patch, created by time and amphibian activity. The shaft of light hit this, and was instantly diverted up and into the channel.

The Grand Equinox of Glisteneratum was on its way.

"What do they mean, 'we offer you our finest'?" Bone's voice was, for once, not rich and fruity.

Jim frowned. "Your guess is as good as mine. Look at them. She's got them in a complete and utter trance."

"Arrr."

"It looks like the same sort of trance that happens to masses of people when they're gathered together. You know, Bone, the sort that the Indian Fakirs do when they perform their rope tricks."

"I wish I had a cigar left. Hello, it looks like Madam Candlehead's going to talk again."

Celestera raised her arm, and the crowd ceased their chanting. Every head was turned to her glowing light.

"Soon, my fellow Atlanteans, the Golden Spirit of Glisteneratum" – she gestured to Sekheret's casket – "will be with us again. As those of thou who are old enough will remember, we have been visited every year by the Golden Spirit. First we were blessed with the Golden One—"

"Glisteneratum," the people chanted at the sarcophagus.

"—and then, shortly after, the Golden Spirit began to grace us with its presence. Today, my people, is indeed a special Equinox. When I was made Keeper of the Sacrarium so many years ago, I was told by Tyra, the retiring Keeper, that there used to be a time when we were able to offer up to the Golden Spirit treasures of such great worth that we could hold our heads high with pride. In those days, many Keepers ago, our people offered the holy Apis Bull – a creature so beautiful and fat that the Spirit was always well pleased."

"Of course!" whispered Jim. "Don't you remember, Bone? The underground tombs at Saqqara? We've always

thought that those huge square sarcophagi were built down there to contain the holy Apis Bulls. Maybe these people – their forebears – were the builders of all that!"

"Mmm," Bone frowned.

"But," Celestera continued, "soon there came a time when there were no longer any Apis Bulls left. The Golden Spirit was not pleased. The Keepers of the Sacrarium have passed down the history of our land through the generations. We have always remembered that it was through the displeasure of the Golden One that our nation came to be placed in this world."

"Glisteneratum, Glisteneratum," came the chant.

"But today, my people, we shall make amends! The Golden Spirit will be well pleased once again! Today we shall offer up another Apis Bull, fully adorned and with extra embellishments!"

The people chanted excitedly.

"What *is* she babbling about? Sub-human stultiloquence, why, I'll bet—"

"Listen!" Jim said. "What's that ringing?" He looked around at Brenda and Doris, and his heart froze. "Bone! They're gone!"

"Good riddance," said Bone, but he frowned all the same.

High above the sarcophagus of Sekheret, a huge bronze bell was swinging back and forth, its peal ringing out and filling every corner of the temple. Celestera was swaying in time to the motion of the bell.

"It is time," she cried, her eyes rolling up behind her

finny eyebrows. "It is time!"

At the back of the temple, six guards opened the enormous doors wide. Every Atlantean turned to face the entrance. The bell ceased its ringing. The only noises to be heard were Cairo Jim's heartbeats, thudding louder than a forest being felled.

Slowly, silently, searingly, the shaft of sunlight was spreading through the streets outside. All of the lamps had been dimmed, both inside the temple and out, and the light from the shaft was becoming brighter and brighter, and faster and faster, as it approached the temple.

It sped straight up the steps, between the dilapidated columns, and into the temple itself!

In the dimness of this vast chamber, its edges were clearly defined, being no wider than a metre and a half. Its crisp goldenness travelled along the central aisle, past the masses of benches, past Glorious, past Celestera, until finally it came to settle perfectly on the serene face carved into the gold of Pharaoh Sekheret's sarcophagus.

Cairo Jim was cleaved down the middle: one half of him was awe-struck at the spectacle he had just witnessed, and the other half tormented wildly by the uncertainty of his friends' whereabouts.

He did not have to wait long to find out where they were, however. Celestera stepped forward and, in a voice like a thousand whirlpools, proclaimed:

"Oh, Mighty Glisteneratum, we lay before you our gifts. Behold the Apis!"

From out of the floor immediately in front of the sarcophagus, a pedestal was rising, slowly and with great ceremony. Standing on top of this pedestal was Brenda the Wonder Camel, with Doris the macaw strapped onto the top of her head, between her ears, like some silvery, feathered ornamental headdress. They came to a stop and were bathed in the golden glow from the light of the Equinox.

"Quaaaooo," snorted Brenda, terror rushing through her nostrils. Doris gave a rocketing screech and tried to flap her wings fiercely, but she had been secured tightly.

"Aaah," wailed Jim.

"Zooks," said Bone. "They're going to be sacrificed!"

Jim was more numb than the Sphinx of Giza.

"And these are not all," Celestera announced as two burly fishmen came forth bearing enormous, glinting scimitars. "Before we spill the blood of the Apis, there will be an entrée of two who have also come from the skies!" She extended her arm to the drapes concealing Jim and Bone.

"Us?" cried Bone. "She's doing us as well? Oh, no, no, no! I'm not ready for the After Life just yet. No, it can't be. I haven't even written Mother a goodbye note. Oh, hoo, hoo, hoo. Arrr. Hoo, hoo, hoo. Oh, Jim, can't we do something?"

It was then that Jim remembered exactly the meaning of the word that described the room in which they now stood, and he almost kicked himself that he hadn't remembered it earlier: a Sacrarium is a place where the

offerings are traditionally kept prior to a ceremony of sacrifice!

The congregation were going into another trance, their incantation rising and falling like a mighty whisper: "Glisteneratum, Glisteneratum, Glisteneratum—"

Two guards were marching purposefully towards the burgundy curtain, coming to take the archaeologists. The two fishmen by the pedestal were sharpening their scimitars on broad leather straps.

"Quaaaooo," Brenda snorted, and Doris cried out:

"Jim! Jim! Reerraaaark! What can we do?"

The archaeologist-poet clenched his fists, the anger at the sight of his two dearest companions in their predicament rising up and smothering any fear he had been feeling. His mind became calm and rational; he let the anger surge through every fibre of his body, turning desperation into motivation. He thought about everything that was happening about him; heard the blubbering of Neptune Bone; watched the two guards drawing closer.

It was then he remembered something Teddy Snorkel had given him.

MEANS OF ESCAPE

"BONE! STOP THAT SNIVELLING and listen to me. The guards'll be here in a few moments—"

"Not me, not me!"

"—but I think there's some hope." Jim reached across to one of the small shoe-shaped lamps resting in an alcove in the wall next to the drapes. The flame in this lamp had burned down very low and, with a quick puff, Jim blew it out completely. He waved it around quickly, giving it a chance to cool (it was not extremely hot as the flame had been low), and turned to Bone. "Do you have that wretched silver cigar-lighter of yours handy?"

Bone wiped away a fat tear. "Arrr," he nodded, reaching down into the inside of his oversized diving suit. "I always keep it on me. A present from Mother."

"Rightio." Jim swiftly concealed the lamp between his two hands. "Bone, you'll have to cooperate with me for once. If my plan works, we may be able to get away."

"Anything, I'll do anything."

"Just keep that lighter handy. When I give the word, you must—"

At that moment, the drapes were hurled aside and the two gigantic guards were standing before them. Neptune Bone whimpered at their size.

They ushered both archaeologists out of the Sacrarium and into the long aisle which led to Brenda, Doris and Sekheret. "The road to ruin," muttered Bone as he trudged along after Jim.

As they approached the altar, Cairo Jim pretended his arm was itchy. He reached around to scratch it (keeping the small lamp carefully concealed in his other hand) and, as inconspicuously as he could, unzipped the pocket behind his elbow. He quickly reached in and fished out five of the oxygen tablets Teddy Snorkel had given him. Then he re-fastened the zipper and stuffed the five tablets as tightly as he could into the lamp. This was the easiest part, as he could hold his hands together in an almost reverent pose, and it looked quite natural considering where they were.

"Keep your fingers crossed, Bone, that my knowledge of chemistry will see us through."

"Arrr," Bone hissed back, the perspiration dripping from his broad forehead and running down into his matted beard.

Jim's brass ring was dangling and trembling and knocking against his knees whenever he took a step, but it was of small concern to him right now.

Finally, after the most agonising walk in memory, they arrived at the pedestal of Brenda and Doris.

"My friends," Jim whispered. "I'm so sorry. Don't give up hope, though; I've a plan up my sleeve."

Doris heard him and her crest feathers stiffened and arched boldly forward, struggling against the confines of

her cranium cover. "I'm right behind you, buddy-boy," she prowked, giving him a wink.

The fear momentarily left Brenda's large eyes, and she gave a reassured and loyal snort. "Quaaooo."

"Oh, woe, woe, a thousand times woe!" moaned Neptune Bone.

"Sh!" hissed Glorious.

"Fellow Atlanteans," proclaimed Celestera, her hands raised high next to her candles, "The moment has arrived. Witness the sacrifice of these beings from the sky!"

The two fishmen moved closer to Jim and Bone, brandishing the glinting scimitars at the captives" throats. Jim whipped out the lamp and, holding it flat in the palm of his hand, pointed it in their direction.

"Now, Bone! Light the wick at the back. Quickly, man!"

Bone's fingers were slippery with anxiety. He held his cigar-lighter close to the lamp wick and struck the flint. It lit straight away.

The wick burnt directly into the lamp and Jim held his breath. "Please," he thought, "please let there be a reaction!"

Suddenly an enormous ball of flame whooshed out from the spouted end of the lamp, straight at the faces of the two fishmen. They recoiled in terror, dropped their scimitars and fled, their finned hands shielding their singed finny eyebrows.

Then Jim's poetry cells welled up beyond his control, and he was blurting:

You think we're beaten, broken, down?
Well, I've got news for you!
You'll wish we'd never seen this town
Before the day is through!

"What in the name of Cousteau?" shouted Celestera, and Jim turned the lamp towards her. Another wall of fire surged out, whooshing towards her candles.

Glorious ducked for cover as her mistress, unable to move speedily because of the great weight on her head, stumbled away from the heat.

"Quick, Bone, grab a scimitar and cut Brenda and Doris loose."

"Arrr." For once, the heat of the situation got to Bone and he cooperated. He swept up the biggest weapon and raised it above his heavy diving helmet. "Tell me to 'shh' now, you fish-faced cauldron of crabbiness," he sneered at Glorious, who was crouching in a corner. Then he sliced through the seaweed ropes that imprisoned Brenda and Doris.

Several burly guards were advancing from the right-hand side of the temple. Jim saw them from the corner of his eye and held the lamp towards them. He gave it a quick jiggle in his hand, and another, even fiercer bank of fire spewed forth at them. They held back, the flames dancing in their scared eyeballs.

"Right, gang," shouted Jim. "Bone and I'll run first, down this aisle. You, Brenda and Doris, bring up the rear. I'll keep those afore at bay with the fire. If they get

too close to the back, Brenda, don't be afraid to lash out with a few good kicks. Stay close, and let's *go!*"

Bone looked out of the face-door of his helmet at the mighty visage of Sekheret. "But, Jim, the doubloons, and those marvellous marbles. They're worth – couldn't we just—?"

"*Come on!*" He grabbed the sleeve of Bone's diving suit and pulled him away.

They hurtled down the central aisle as though they were on wheels. The congregation at first tried to crowd them off, to bar their way by cutting their path, but Jim gave a quick jiggle of the lamp and the wild flames that erupted and shot out soon dispersed everyone from their immediate route.

At last they were at the double doors. Jim gave a final burst of flame at the people within before joining his companions on the outside. As soon as he was out, Brenda slammed one door shut, putting all her weight behind it, and Bone did likewise with the other. Jim slammed a barricade post into place across the doors.

The Equinox light came to a stop against the heavy doors, and shimmered as if it were perplexed.

They all stood puffing on the platform at the top of the steps which led down into the central courtyard. Brenda could still feel something nudging uncomfortably against her nether hump, inside her diving suit, but she wasn't about to do anything about it now. Bone leaned against one of the half-broken columns and took off his diving helmet. "Phew! What now?"

Jim stared ahead. "That way, I think. We've got to get back to the channel. It's the only way." He looked nervously at the barricade post. "It's not going to last for long," he said, hearing the groan of timber.

"Uh-oh," squawked Doris, pointing with her silvery wing. "Looks like trouble."

At the far end of the courtyard a wild horde of shouting Atlanteans was advancing towards them. Many of them carried spears and scimitars and primitive-looking coat hangers.

"Arrrr," wailed Bone, putting his helmet back on again. The column against which he was leaning shifted with his weight.

Behind Brenda, the double doors of the temple started heaving. "Quaaaooo," she snorted desperately as they started to break open.

Jim jiggled the lamp and held it at the doors, but the energy supply had depleted; no flames shot out. He jiggled it again and again, but it was no use.

"What'll we do, Jim, what'll we do?" Doris screeched.

Jim reached into the pocket behind his elbow and withdrew another five oxygen tablets. These he quickly inserted into the lamp, being careful not to burn his fingers against the hot clay inside it. And then an idea came to him.

"Bone," he shouted, as the doors heaved again and the hordes rushed closer, "d'you remember at archaeology school, in our Jungle Expeditions classes,

how they taught us to run along on top of a moving log?"

"Er – yes," lied Bone, who had skipped those classes to sell plastic scarabs to the tourists.

The doors were almost opened wide enough to let people out of the temple. "Right," said Jim breathlessly. "Push that column over. It's loose at the bottom, shouldn't be too much effort."

"What've we got to lose?" scowled Bone, putting his shoulder to it.

Brenda quickly came to help him. Together they heaved and grunted and the column began to teeter. Another huge push and it toppled, falling heavily, and chipping only slightly, onto the top of the steps.

"Right!" Jim yelled above the noise of the approaching multitude. "All aboard!"

Brenda scrambled up on the side of the column as it rolled uncertainly back and forth on the top step. In another second or two it would roll off and down the steps. She lowered her hoof to Jim, who quickly latched onto it and pulled himself up to join her. Doris flew to rest on the shoulder of his silver suit. Bone hesitated.

"Quick, Bone, we'll need you to light the wick!"

Brenda offered her hoof again and Bone grabbed it. Up he came onto the side of the column like a fattish spider.

The doors burst open with a noise like a cannon, and Jim, balancing as best he could on the ever-quickly-rolling column, held the lamp in the direction of the congregation who were spilling out at them. "Quick, the

wick!" he shouted at Bone.

Bone was having trouble keeping his footing as the column wheeled back and forth, but he reached across and sparked open his lighter, setting it against the wick. The flames burst forth, stronger and brighter than before, and Jim pointed them at the marauders.

There was a massive shriek, and they fell back inside the temple.

"Right, Brenda, Bone, on the count of three – you hold on tight, Doris, my dear, beat your wings a bit for extra aerodynamics – ready, all? One, two, *three*!"

They began to walk forwards very slowly and, as they took each step, the column started to roll. Off the top step it came, down onto the next step with a huge bang, then down to the next and the next and the next; *bang*, roll, *bang*, roll, *bang*, roll.

"Keep the pace up. Okay, we're almost at the bottom. As soon as we hit the courtyard, *run like billy-o*!"

"Arrrr," wailed Bone, wishing that he had pursued a career as a florist.

The Atlanteans ahead stopped approaching, and stood in silence for a few moments as the column, with its strange clockwork-like motor of running humans and quadruped and bird, began tearing in their direction. Then the steamroller-type thing thunked down onto the flat courtyard and its pace accelerated markedly. Jim jiggled the lamp as he ran along the top of the column, keeping pace with Brenda and Bone, and gigantic flames leapt out as though they were from the very jaws of a dragon!

The horde of Atlanteans threw up their fins and disbanded, running as fast as they could out of harm's way. Many of them darted up laneways which led off the courtyard; others jumped onto window ledges or plinths that held statues; some of the less quick-thinking ones remained in the path of the roaring, fire-breathing column, trying to outrun it, but to no avail – they soon threw themselves onto the ground, only centimetres from its path.

On and on it careered, through the courtyard, past the hippodrome (strangely quiet on this holiest of days), down the main thoroughfare that Jim, Doris, Brenda and Bone had all been dragged along in their nets. All the while, the archaeologists and Brenda ran and bounded, never missing a beat (even Bone, under the worst pressure he had ever suffered in his life, managed to keep the pace), and Doris gave them all extra velocity through her beautifully measured wingbeats. Still, the brass rings dangled wildly at the ends of the strings on the Teddy Snorkel suits.

At last they were approaching the outskirts of the city. As the column began to arrive at the base of the steep hill which led up almost to the top of the broad dome of the submarine cavern, Jim gave the signal for everyone to jump off.

"End of the road! All off!"

They jumped sideways off the rotating vehicle, and came to rest in rough heaps on the pebbly ground. The column continued rolling of its own accord.

"Are you all right, Brenda?" flapped Doris, hovering above the dishevelled Wonder Camel.

"Quaaooo," snorted Brenda, shaking her head in a circle and squirming at the uncomfortableness near her nether hump.

Jim sprang to his feet and helped the weighted-down Bone up as well. "Right," he puffed, looking behind them to make sure they were not being pursued. "It's up and over this hill. The waterline is down the other side. Once we pass through that, we just have to swim like rockets to the surface." He threw the extinguished lamp to the ground.

"Arrr. I can barely move in these lead boots."

"Stop whining, you gasbag," Doris screeched.

"We'll pull you up, Bone, don't fret."

Together they half-sped, half-plodded up the rough hill, sweating and grunting as they hauled the overweighted Bone behind them. Finally, after what seemed hours, they were at the top.

Looking down the other side, they saw the thin, almost invisible line hanging in the air, separating the dry world from the oceaned.

"Come on, downwards and onwards!" Cairo Jim began to scuttle towards the waterline.

"Halt!" Bone cried, and Jim stopped in his tracks.

"What's wrong?" squawked Doris, glancing over her wing at the crest of the hill.

"There's one slight problem." Bone's face was glistening with perspiration through the face-door of his

gigantic helmet. "My oxygen hose was destroyed by those barbarians when I arrived. I'll never make it to the top without air. I may as well be dead now."

Jim reached into the pocket behind his elbow and extricated the last four oxygen tablets. He held them out in the palm of his hand. "All's not lost. Look, there's enough left for us to have one each. Just suck on it slowly, Bone. Hopefully it'll last you until you hit the surface."

Jim frowned slightly and turned to Doris and Brenda. "My friends, we'll have to operate on half of what we had when we came down. Take it slowly and carefully. With fortune behind us, we should make it."

"Quaaooo," snorted Brenda.

"Reeeeraaark!" screamed Doris. "Jim, coming up the hill behind us! Plankton men!"

A battalion of the amphibious plankton men were swarming after them.

"Right," Jim cried, "now we've really got to move!"

With primeval malevolence, Captain Neptune Bone reached out and snatched all the oxygen tablets from Jim's opened hand. "I'll move, all right, you credulous cretin!" He began to hurtle down the slope towards the waterline.

"But, Bone, that's all we've got!"

"Tough nut, eh?" The pudgy man threw the handful into his mouth and clanged his face-door shut. Then he dived headfirst through the waterline and disappeared in a bubbly blur.

THINGS ON THE SURFACE

"JIM, JIM, they're getting closer!"

Brenda stomped her hoofs urgently.

"Rark! What do we do?"

"I have no idea," replied Jim, for once in his life absolutely, hopelessly, stumped.

The shouting was growing louder, uglier, turning into a rising growl, as the plankton men rushed to the top of the hill.

Jim's mind was pulsating against his temples as he tried to work out what to do. Should they try to dive through the waterline, and hope that they could hold their breaths long enough until they reached the top of the Red Sea? Should they try and confront their pursuers? Should they simply give in?

Just then Doris gave a squawk. "Brenda! This is no time to have a wrestle!"

The Wonder Camel had gently pushed the macaw down to the ground, and was pinioning her there, hoof against the bird's silvery belly. Doris was struggling to get free as Brenda slid her around so that the top of her head was pointed down towards the waterline.

"*Raaaaaark!*"

With her supple lips, Brenda brought Doris's goggles

down so that they covered the macaw's eyes. Then, before there were any further protests, Brenda locked her jaws around Doris's brass ring – the same infernal ring that had been dangling like a broken feather ever since she had put the diving suit on – and gave it, and the string, a sharp tug.

Brenda quickly let go, and the brave and noble macaw went shooting off down the slope, as though she was a bullet let loose from a pistol. Down she plummeted, breaking the waterline so speedily that it barely rippled. Upon contact with the water, her silver diving suit lost half its actual weight, and she vanished instantly.

"Brenda, you brilliant—"

Jim got no further; Brenda flipped him onto his stomach and quickly pulled his brass ring. Off he shot, pulling down his goggles and gulping every molecule of air he could get into his lungs.

The plankton men came up and over the top of the hill like a spreading oil slick. Brenda threw herself to the ground, and was getting herself into a suitable contortion so that she could reach her own brass ring when a flat, finny hand slammed down on her nether hump.

This was the hump around which she had been feeling so much unusual discomfort, and the hand made her even more aware of it. She gave an angry snort, kicked out at the rude plankton man, and sent him flying. Another assailant was rushing at her, an enormous trident held before him as he aimed it straight at her snout.

178

With true Wonder, Brenda stretched her head beneath her belly, bit hard at the brass ring, and extended her neck sharply to its full length. And she was off!

The plankton men scattered as the huge Bactrian beast powered down to the waterline. Some of them made vain attempts to chase her, but they needn't have bothered; in a blink of time, she had entered the watery channel.

Inspector Mustafa Kuppa had just polished his Hollywood-style sun-spectacles and wiped his brow with his handkerchief when he saw something very strange indeed.

Erupting like a water-logged volcano, the Red Sea shot out a small, silvery object. Up it rose into the air, fluttering and flapping, as the surface of the water beneath it bubbled as though it was boiling.

Kuppa blinked and watched as the silver thing hovered for a moment in the air. He drew up his binoculars and saw that the thing was in the form of a bird: a bird encased, so it seemed, in silver foil. It shook its beaked head a few times, and flew over to the shore.

"Boy," thought Doris, "Teddy Snorkel sure can pack a punch!" She started to simultaneously peel herself out of the silver suit and kiss the sand with her beak. "Terra firma!" she cooed. "Never was a bird happier to see sand!"

Suddenly another silvery missile caught Kuppa's binoculared attention. Long, sleek and human in shape, it too shot up several metres out of the water and into the air, before falling down beneath the surface again. A

few seconds passed, and the silvery shape bobbed up like a bottle, and began swimming to the sand dunes.

"Well," said Kuppa aloud, "if this isn't Jim of Cairo and his companions, I'll be Zasu Pitts."

Then a third, more cumbersome, silvery thing was spewed into the air. It splashed down loudly and began a gentle camel-paddle to join the other two things.

Jim peeled off his cranium cover and threw it onto the sand, before throwing his arms around his best feathered friend. "My dear, we made it. We're here!" A tear welled up in his eye, and he pulled out his special desert sun-spectacles and put them on to hide it.

"Rark! Thanks to Brenda the Bold!" The macaw nuzzled against Jim's neck. In a second, her beak thwanged up against her eyes, and Jim had to reset it for her.

Brenda lumbered up to join them, water gushing from her belt and the folds in her diving suit. The archaeologist and macaw looked at her for a long, silent moment; then they embraced her so tightly her eyelashes tingled.

"Quaaaoooo!"

Much to Doris's embarrassment, Jim spurted out a poem for their four-legged companion:

The very snort of you,
makes us forget, we two,
the dreadful things and worlds and scares
that we've just been through.
You've saved our feathers, skin and bacon

you've brought us up all trumps,
I'm surely not mistaken,
we love your beautiful humps—

"Cairo Jim! What an earnest, though I must say not unexpected, pleasure to meet you once again."

"Inspector Kuppa!" Jim patted Brenda's neck and turned to face the Antiquities Squad member. "We've just had a little outing."

"Hmmm." Kuppa blew a pipe-full of smoke into the timid breeze. "You didn't by any chance happen to come across Captain Neptune Bone on your travels, did you?"

"Oh, my goodness!" Jim had forgotten about the guttersnipe.

A grotty bundle of feathers hopped out from behind a sand dune and fixed them all with red, haughty eyeballs. "He's dead, isn't he?" wailed Desdemona. "I knew it. As dead as a drowned doorknob. Oh, hoo, hoo, hoo!"

"Desdemona," soothed Jim. "We don't know that for certain."

"Quaaooo!"

"Reerrk! Look, Brenda's seen something." Everyone looked out in the direction in which Brenda was indicating with her front right hoof.

Off in the middle of the Red Sea, a giant, billowing, shiny black mass was splashing and flailing.

Kuppa raised his binoculars and focused. "It looks like a diving suit, although it appears to have been filled

with enough air to float a dirigible."

"That's what he gets for being a greedy-guts," Doris whispered to Jim and Brenda.

"Wait a momentum," Kuppa continued, "it's opening the face-door in its helmet. Ah! I knew it! It is none other than that felon, that scoundrel, that bucket of rudeness, Neptune Bone!"

"Oh, my Captain, my Captain!" Desdemona was shaking so much, many of her fleas were being evicted from her feathers. "Hold on! Help is on its way! I'll just rev up the Beastie!" Away she swooped before anyone had a chance to stop her.

The rubber Beast of the Red Sea chugged out from its mooring spot and sped to the floating archaeologist. Desdemona drew the vessel alongside and, with her sharp beak, bit through Bone's diving suit until he was able to climb out of it and up into the belly of the fake monster.

"Stop! Stop in the name of all that is Antiquity!" bellowed Kuppa.

Bone's smirking face appeared in the doorway in the side of the Beast. He had removed his helmet and was smoking a cigar as though his very life depended on it. After a few maniacal puffs, he took it from his mouth and raised a megaphone to his lips. "So," he declaimed across the water. "I live to fight another day. Arrrrrr."

"Come here this instant!" Kuppa shouted, his voice becoming high-pitched and shrill.

"You come and get me, Kuppa. You deluded little

man, you've got nothing on me! Full steam ahead, Desdemona, and stop kissing my kneecaps." The Beast started gathering speed. "Oh, and Jim?"

Cairo Jim waited, as Bone's face leered out. "Yes, Bone?"

"I'll send you a bill for my dry-cleaning. Arrrrrrrrr!"

The Beast started to grow smaller.

"Well," Jim shrugged. "I guess that's that."

"Maybe not," Doris squawked. "Look!"

The Red Sea was rippling close by Bone's Beast. The ripples were small at first, but were growing bigger and bigger, and radiating wider and wider. Then a huge series of bubbles the size of bowling-balls exploded to the surface.

Inside the Beast, Bone fell back against the wall. "What in the name of Poseidon?"

"Look," cried Kuppa. "It is the mighty Kraken! It has risen! Oh, where is my camera?"

The dark and slabbery creature reared up out of the water, the sunlight glinting off its hide for the first time in nearly three hundred years. A definite aroma of sweet plums filled the air.

"Smell that?" shouted Kuppa. "Those sweet plums! Do you know what that means?"

"No," said Jim, whose knowledge of ancient sea serpents was not prolific.

"It means the Kraken is in love! I have read about this. My cousin wrote a respected tome on Leviathans of the Deep, you know. The Kraken is looking for a mate!"

"And I think he's found it," Doris screeched. The walloping sea creature had seen the pathetic rubberised miniature version, and had altered its course most obviously. As it pursued its intended love-mate, the smell of sweet plums grew stronger and sweeter.

Bone saw and smelled all of this through a hole near his serpent's tail. "Top speed, top speed, you loitering lintball!" he wailed, scratching at his fingernails.

"We're doing top speed now, you old windbag," spat Desdemona.

"Open her up! Let's get out of here! Motherrrrrrrrr!"

With great turbulence the Red Sea swirled.

"So," frowned Mustafa Kuppa, as the two beasts sailed off into the sunset, "he gets away again. From me at least. But I shall meet up with him one day soon, you are my witness to that, Cairo Jim."

"One day, things will be truly sour for him," Jim said.

Kuppa extended his hand and Jim shook it. "Now I must get back to Cairo, to Maxwell House. I should very much appreciate it if you would drop in some time soon and tell me of your escapade, for my report. I should be *most interested*."

"I will," said Jim. "As soon as we've visited Gerald Perry at the Old Relics Society."

"Very good. Until then." He nodded and made his way back to his squad car.

"Jim, Jim, look at this!"

Doris had been helping Brenda out of her diving suit and only now did the Wonder Camel discover the

cause of her nether hump discomfort. Doris held up the tarnished brass plate that had fallen into Brenda's suit the night Doris had stirred in her sleep and knocked it off the bench.

"Quaaaooo," snorted Brenda, relieved that it was not a new hump springing up, as she had been fearing. Two humps were quite enough for her; anything surplus she considered to be ostentatious.

"A souvenir," Doris said, holding it above her beak. "Of our seaside holiday."

"Well, plonk a bucket on my head at a rakish angle and call me Nefertiti," laughed Cairo Jim.

It was only much later, when they were heading back to the Valley of the Kings, that they noticed that the small pattern inlaid into the centre of the tarnished brass plate was actually a stained gold doubloon, bearing a sovereign's head and the inscription:

MONTE CARLO 1829.

THE END

Swoggle me sideways! Unearth more thrilling mysteries of history starring Cairo Jim, Doris, and Brenda the Wonder Camel – **THE CAIRO JIM CHRONICLES**

CAIRO JIM ON THE TRAIL TO CHACHA MUCHOS

Why did an ancient Peruvian tribe dance themselves to death? Can that well-known archaeologist and little-known poet Cairo Jim uncover the secrets of ChaCha Muchos before the evil Captain Bone... And will Jim *ever* get any poetry published? Find out in his first flabbergasting adventure!

CAIRO JIM IN SEARCH OF MARTENARTEN

Does the lost tomb of Pharaoh Martenarten spell doom for Cairo Jim? What lies beyond the Door of Death? Could it, in fact, be doom? And is the world really ready for a pigeon-based fast food chain... Find out in the second scintillating tale of Cairo Jim!

CAIRO JIM AND THE ALABASTRON OF FORGOTTEN GODS

Can Cairo Jim recover the Alabastron of Forgotten Gods in time to save the world? What *is* an alabastron, anyway? Is Euripides Doodah getting tired of people saying "My, oh my, what a wonderful day"? All will be revealed in Cairo Jim's fourth fulminating exploit!

The Cairo Jim Chronicles, read by Geoffrey McSkimming, are available on CD from Bolinda Audio Books! See **www.bolinda.com** for details.